TALISMAN

the MOONCAKE of CHANG-O

Collect all four thrilling
Talisman adventures!

The Tears of Isis
The Mooncake of Chang-O
The Amulet of Quilla
The Elephant of Parvati

TALISMAN

THE MOONCAKE OF CHANG-O

ALLAN FREWIN JONES

Hodder
Children's
Books

A division of Hodder Headline Limited

For Amber
Who told me about the Talismans
and showed me where to find them.

A Catalogue record for this book is available from
the British Library

ISBN 0 340 88225 5

Typeset in Baskerville by Avon DataSet Ltd,
Bidford-on-Avon, Warwickshire

Printed and bound in Great Britain by
Bookmarque Ltd, Croydon, Surrey

The paper and board used in this paperback by Hodder
Children's Books are natural recyclable products made from
wood grown in sustainable forests. The manufacturing
processes conform to the environmental regulations
of the country of origin.

Hodder Children's Books
a division of Hodder Headline Ltd
338 Euston Road
London NW1 3BH

Prologue

' "In ancient days in China, it was said that ten suns lived in the giant Lau Shang tree which grew in the Heavenly Lands away beyond the Eastern Horizon. These ten suns were the offspring of the Sky God, Di Jun, and the Goddess, Xi He. Their mother decreed that only one sun should burn in the sky at a time, and arranged the order in which her offspring would cross the heavens, each taking their turn in Di Jun's chariot. But the unruly suns became discontented with the discipline their mother imposed on them, and they muttered together and came up with a plan to break free of their tedious duties.

' "One morning, all ten suns appeared together

blazing defiantly in the sky. They ignored their mother when she called for them to return to the tree. They did not even heed the mighty voice of Di Jun, their heavenly father – they were free at last, and they were determined to remain so.

' "At first, the people of Earth greeted the ten suns with delight, but soon their crops began to wither under the fierce heat, and their rivers dried up and their lands became parched. The Emperor of China implored Di Jun to help the people and to restore the old order.

' "Di Jun sent emissaries to Earth – a mighty archer, named Hou-Yi, and his beautiful wife, Chang-O. Di Jun gave Hou-Yi a red bow and a quiver full of white arrows. With these he hoped Hou-Yi would be able to frighten the ten rebellious suns back to their duties. But when Hou-Yi saw the scorched and thirsty earth, he grew angry, and one by one he shot down nine of the suns from the sky.

' "The people were delighted and proclaimed Hou-Yi a hero, but Di Jun was angry at the deaths of his suns, and he condemned Hou-Yi and Chang-O to remain on Earth and to become mortal.

' "But Hou-Yi chafed under the yoke of mortality.

He went into the Uttermost West and sought the Queen Goddess who lived on Mount Kunlun. She gave him a pill of everlasting life, and told him to prepare himself with twelve months of prayer and fasting before taking the pill.

' "Returning to his home, Hou-Yi hid the pill in the rafters of the roof and began his long preparations. One night, Chang-O was awoken by the delightful fragrance of flowers. She rose and followed a single white moonbeam which shone out from the pill. Chang-O picked up the pill and swallowed it – and found that she could fly.

' "She flew through the house and out into the lotus-scented garden, singing joyfully as she soared beneath the full moon. Her husband awoke, and when he realised what Chang-O had done, he became terribly angry. Chang-O fled her husband's wrath, but he pursued her over mountains and plains, through bamboo forests and across great rivers, until in her fear, she flew up to the moon, seeking refuge.

' "Her only companion on the moon was a magical hare who pounded medicinal herbs with a mortar and pestle. Regretting her actions, and seeking to appease her husband, Chang-O coughed up half the pill. She then commanded the hare to pound up the half-pill and to make of it a new pill which she could take back to Hou-Yi.

' "Each year in China, at the Festival of the Moon, the people eat mooncakes to symbolise the pill made by the hare and to honour the moon-goddess, Chang-O." '

Olivia Christie stopped reading and looked up from the book, her blue eyes shining. 'Well,' she said, 'what do you make of that?'

Josh Welles smiled. 'Nice story, Olly,' he replied, glancing up from his laptop computer. 'What happened when Chang-O gave Hou-Yi the pill back? Did he become immortal again?'

'I don't know,' Olly said. 'I haven't read that far.'

Twelve-year-old Olly and her best friend, Josh – who was only two weeks younger – were seated side by side in a large passenger aircraft. The screen of Josh's laptop showed a map of Asia. A red line indicated their flight-path. Their party had boarded a plane at London Heathrow before dawn that morning. A rapid change at Paris, just as the sun was rising, had brought them aboard their present aircraft for the ten-hour flight to Beijing in China.

They had been in the air for five hours now, and according to Josh's calculations, were flying high over central Asia with half the flight still to complete. But the Chinese capital city was not their final destination. After a night in a hotel, they would be taking another plane south-west into the very heartland of China – to Sechuan Province and the ancient city of Chengdu. There, they would begin the final leg of their mammoth journey to the ancient ruins that had recently been revealed along the banks of the mighty Minjiang River.

Olly's father was the renowned archaeologist, Professor Kenneth Christie. The Chinese authorities had especially requested his presence at this historic dig, and Olly was travelling with him. Her mother had died two years ago, and Olly frequently accompanied her father on his international expeditions, looked after and tutored by her formidable grandmother, Audrey Beckmann.

Professor Christie's assistant, a brilliant archaeological student called Jonathan Welles, was Josh's twenty-year-old brother. Their mother was the famous movie actress, Natasha Welles. Her career did not provide Josh with a very stable home-life, so it had been agreed that he should accompany his brother and the Christies on their continent-hopping adventures – which worked out well, because he and Olly had soon become the best of friends.

Olly peered out of the small window. The aeroplane hung in a clear blue sky above an endless panorama of barren, snow-capped mountains. As she stared down at the breathtaking but forbidding wild-lands of the Alatau Mountains, Olly felt the wonderful knot of excitement in her stomach that always accompanied the start of a new quest.

It was only a few weeks ago that they had been in the Valley of the Kings in Egypt, excavating the ancient tomb of Pharaoh Setiankhra. Olly still couldn't quite believe that she and Josh had actually been the ones to find the golden room deep under the cliffs – the room known as the Chamber of Light. In spite of ancient booby-traps and perilous rock-falls, the two friends had brought out the beautiful twin sapphires that formed the Tears of Isis – one of the legendary Talismans of the Moon.

If the legends were true, then the Talismans of

the Moon had been fashioned millennia ago by moon-priests of ancient civilisations in different parts of the world. Each culture shaped its own talisman, and it was said that if they were all brought together at the right time and place, then great wonders would be revealed.

In the course of his recent archaeological investigations, Professor Christie had found evidence that the talismans might be more than mere legend. Ever since, he had been determined to track them all down and unlock their secrets.

Olly breathed a sigh of pure joy and settled back in her seat, thrilled to be on a new adventure. She turned over the page of her book on Chinese mythology and read on.

' "According to some versions of the myth," ' she related to Josh, ' "the hare is still pounding away on the pill. But other versions say that the hare completed the new pill, and that it hardened into a disc of pure moonstone." ' She frowned. 'What's moonstone?'

Josh opened a search engine on the laptop and tapped at the keyboard. 'Here we are,' he said a moment later. 'Moonstone is a semi-precious gem with a white or blue sheen. It reflects light in a distinctive shimmering way. It is found in Brazil, India, the USA, Madagascar and Mexico.' He grinned. 'And on the moon,' he joked.

Olly laughed. 'In this other version of the myth, Chang-O took the pill down to Earth and started searching for Hou-Yi, but she never found him. It's said that she still has the moonstone with her in her final resting place – which, according to legend, is the lost city of Yueliang-Chengshi.' She looked at Josh. 'And Dad is pretty convinced that the moonstone – wherever it really came from – is the legendary Mooncake of Chang-O, one of the Talismans of the Moon.'

Jonathan Welles's face appeared over the back of his seat, his long, light-brown fringe falling into his warm brown eyes as always. 'How's it going?' he asked. 'Having fun?'

'I was just reading Josh the myth of Chang-O,' Olly told him. She looked up at Jonathan curiously. 'What makes Dad think we're going to find the talisman at this particular dig?' she asked.

'Only a few years ago a great lost palace was found not far from this city,' Jonathan explained. 'And lots of very interesting discoveries were made . . .'

'Didn't the professor tell you about the map that was found?' came Audrey Beckmann's voice from her seat across the aisle. Olly's sixty-three-year-old grandmother was a tall, elegant woman with grey hair cut into a neat bob. She supervised the day-to-day running of the small party – ensuring that the other-worldly professor ate properly and had clean clothes to put on, as well as keeping a stern but affectionate eye on Olly and Josh.

'I don't think he mentioned any maps to me,' Olly said. 'But you know Dad. When he's working he goes into a world of his own and forgets all about ordinary things like talking to people.'

'I know the map you mean,' Josh broke in. 'They found part of an ancient map carved on an earthenware pot. It seemed to show that the lost city of Yueliang-Chengshi was to the south, somewhere along the course of the Minjiang River between the modern-day towns of Leshan and Yibin.'

Olly frowned at him. 'How do you know that?'

Josh laughed. 'Jonathan told me,' he replied.

'Well, you might have mentioned it!' Olly sighed.

'What's all the noise?' asked a new voice to the conversation. Professor Christie's head appeared around the side of his seat, his greying hair an untidy thatch, his bright eyes glinting over half-moon glasses. 'I can't hear myself think with all this chattering.'

'We were just discussing the finding of the map, Kenneth,' Audrey Beckmann explained.

The professor nodded enthusiastically. 'At first I was worried that the map was just symbolic – that it didn't show real things in their real places. But the findings at this new site, where we will be working, suggest otherwise.'

'What findings?' Olly asked. She loved hearing the excitement in her father's voice when he talked about his work, and she was quick to take advantage of having distracted him from his reading.

'An inscription found among the ruins indicates that these might be the remains of the lost city of Yueliang-Chengshi itself. If so, then it's more or less exactly where the terracotta map indicated it would be,' Professor Christie explained.

'The inscription reads, *Here Hou-Yi finally lost Chang-O – she who fled to the moon*,' added Jonathan.

'And the myth says that Chang-O's final resting place was in Yueliang-Chengshi!' Olly exclaimed in delight. 'I'd say that was pretty good evidence.'

'Let's hope so,' said the professor, turning back to his work. 'And let's hope we can find more evidence before the river rises again.'

The teeming waters of the Minjiang flowed down from the mountains of the Tibetan Plateau, until they spilled at last into the huge Yangtze River and began the epic two-thousand-kilometre journey to the distant East China Sea. But the rain had failed that spring and the river had dwindled to half its normal size, revealing broad banks that had not been dry land for a thousand years. And from the mud and silt of those exposed riverbanks, the eroded ruins of ancient buildings jutted like broken brown teeth.

The Chinese authorities had invited a few internationally-renowned archaeologists to come and excavate the site – but it was a race against time. When the rain finally did come, the mountains would empty millions of tons of floodwater down into the valley of the Minjiang River and the ruins would be lost again.

Olly took another look out of the window. The vast mountain range still stretched away beneath them. 'This is taking for ever,' she said. 'I want to get there and start searching for the talisman!'

'I think not,' her gran said firmly. 'On this trip, I'm determined to make sure you two behave yourselves and keep out of mischief.'

'Spoilsport,' Olly said with a grin. She exchanged a secret glance with Josh, knowing that once they were on site, he would be as eager as her to join in the hunt for the fabled Mooncake of Chang-O.

Chapter One

The Sacred Mountain

It was late in the afternoon of the following day and they were airborne again.

They had landed at Beijing International Airport at three in the morning, local time, disorientated by the shift in time zones and exhausted by over eleven hours of travelling. Official cars had whisked them to the airport hotel for the night. Then, far too early the next morning for Olly's liking, they had been roused from their beds to take the internal flight to Sechuan Province.

A third, much smaller aircraft was waiting for their party when they touched down at Shangliu Airport several hours later. It was an elderly twin-prop plane, chartered locally, and only just large enough to take the small party and their baggage.

The difference was dramatic. The plane flew low, hugging the land, the whole fuselage vibrating to the roar of the engines. There were no luxuries on this flight and the seats were hard and narrow – but Olly loved it. It made her feel as if the adventure had really begun.

She and Josh leant together to look out of the window as the scenery passed swiftly below them – the landscape changing from rice paddies to bamboo forests and then to orchards and cultivated fields of corn and wheat. They pointed down excitedly to towns and villages of traditional wooden houses with roofs of orange tiles or tan-coloured bamboo thatch. And all the while, the foothills of the vast Tibetan Plateau drew closer, and the land began to rise and fall in deeply forested hills and lush valleys. Occasionally on a wooded hillside, they would glimpse the elegant, curved roof of an isolated Buddhist temple, emerging from the trees like something from a bygone age. And in the distance, they could see the mountains looming on the horizon.

Jonathan leant over to speak to the two friends. 'We should see the river soon,' he told them. 'I've just been talking to the pilot. We'll be approaching the site from the north, following the course of the Minjiang.'

It was only a couple of minutes later that Olly and Josh caught sight of the river. Here, the effects of the drought were alarmingly obvious – the once ample waterway had dwindled to less than half its usual width, shrinking to a murky brown thread no more than ten metres across, that ran between deep sloping banks of cracked earth.

An ancient irrigation system kept the cultivated land green and growing, but in places, entire stretches of the countryside were no more than parched brown earth from which grey rocks jutted like bare bones.

The sight pricked Olly's conscience. She looked round at Jonathan. 'All I've been thinking about is how great it's going to be for us to see the old ruins,' she said sadly. 'I didn't really consider what it must be like for the people around here.'

Jonathan nodded. 'They're just about surviving at the moment,' he replied. 'But if the drought goes on for much longer things will get very bad for them.'

Josh frowned. 'It gives you mixed feelings, doesn't

it?' he said. 'I mean, we'd like the rain to hold off till we can find out everything there is to know about the ruins, but at the same time, you can't help hoping the rain comes as soon as possible.'

Olly smiled ruefully. 'Let's hope there are plenty of diggers on site,' she declared. 'That way, we can get the work done really quickly – and then it can rain as much as it likes.' She looked at Jonathan. 'Who's in charge down there?'

'Professor Andryanova,' Jonathan told her. 'He's Russian – very well thought of by a lot of people.' He leant closer and dropped his voice. 'But just between the three of us, the professor doesn't think much of him.'

Josh looked surprised. 'Isn't he very good, then?' he asked.

'He's good,' Jonathan said. 'He would never have been appointed team-leader otherwise. But he has a reputation for cutting corners to get quick results. And he's a great self-publicist who tends to turn a dig into something of a media circus. Fortunately, the man who's co-funding the dig with the Chinese authorities has insisted on minimum publicity.'

'Who exactly *is* putting up the money?' Olly enquired. 'Gran told me it was an American billionaire.' She looked sharply at Jonathan. 'You don't think it might be Ethan Cain, do you?'

Jonathan gave a soft laugh. 'No, I don't,' he replied. 'And even if it was, I thought we'd cleared up that misunderstanding you had with him in Egypt.' He put his hand on Olly's shoulder. 'Trust me,' he said, 'Ethan Cain is not out to steal the Talismans of the Moon from under your father's nose – and he never was!'

Olly and Josh said nothing – they knew better than to bring up their deeply-held suspicions about the superficially charming Californian billionaire. They were convinced that Ethan Cain had been behind various criminal activities that had dogged the hunt for the Tears of Isis. But no one believed them, and what made things even more awkward was that the wealthy computer genius was actually dating Josh's mother.

'So, who *is* paying for all this?' Josh asked.

'A man named Augustus Bell,' Jonathan said. 'From what I've heard, he's a Texan oil baron with plenty of cash to spare. He's not known in the usual archaeological circles, so I suspect he's funding the dig in order to buy himself into history.'

'Oh, I get it,' Olly put in. 'Everything we find will end up in the Augustus Bell wing of a Chinese museum somewhere.'

Jonathan laughed. 'Something like that,' he agreed. He nodded towards the window. 'Keep your eyes peeled. You should see something pretty spectacular shortly,' he said, and then he moved back to his own seat.

'So, Ethan is definitely not involved in any way?' Olly whispered to Josh.

He shook his head. 'When Mum called us from location in Acapulco the other day, I asked her whether Ethan had shown any interest in the ruins. She told me he was up to his eyes in work in California and hadn't even mentioned them to her.'

'Good!' Olly said emphatically. 'The further Ethan Cain is from here, the better I like it.'

'Shhh!' hissed Josh, glancing over his shoulder. 'If your gran hears you saying stuff like that, we'll get another lecture about not accusing innocent people of being criminals.'

Olly nodded and turned to stare down out of the window. 'Wow!' she exclaimed, all thoughts of Ethan Cain driven from her head.

Josh leant over her shoulder. 'Wow!' he agreed breathlessly.

Here, the river was lined by tall cliffs of rust-coloured stone. Carved in the solid rock-face was a huge statue of a man, seated, with his massive feet planted firmly apart and his hands resting on his knees. His hair was sculpted into a top-knot and he gazed serenely over the river from between thickets of tall trees that grew around his enormous shoulders. Also shrouded by the lofty trees was the rooftop of a huge building – a monastery – which dominated the cliff top.

'Look at the people down there,' Olly said, staring down at the small shapes clustered around the feet of the statue. 'They're tiny!'

'They just *look* tiny,' Josh responded, 'because the statue is over seventy metres tall. It's the Grand Buddha,' he continued. 'It was carved during the Tang Dynasty in the eighth century.'

Olly looked at him. 'You're beginning to sound like a tour guide,' she said with a laugh. 'I hope you're not expecting to get paid for all this info.'

'No, it's all free,' Josh replied. 'I've been looking stuff up on the Internet,' he explained. 'You know I like to find out as much as I can about the places

19

we visit. The next big thing we see will be the sacred mountain.'

'It's called Si-Houzai-Shan,' Olly told him with a grin. 'See? I know some stuff myself. And the place where we're going to be digging is in a bend of the river, right beside the mountain.'

'But do you know what the mountain's name means?' Josh asked.

Olly frowned, trying to remember. 'Dad did tell me,' she said thoughtfully. 'It's something to do with fire.'

'Dead-fire-mountain,' Josh declared. 'Si-Houzai-Shan is an extinct volcano.'

' "Extinct" means totally dead, doesn't it?' Olly queried anxiously. 'I don't fancy hanging out near a volcano that might go off.'

'Actually I asked Ang-Lun about that the last time I e-mailed him,' Josh told her. 'He said it hasn't erupted for hundreds of thousands of years – so I think we're pretty safe.'

Ang-Lun was the twelve-year-old son of a Chinese archaeologist, Doctor Feng Zhe-Hui – who was a close colleague of Olly's father and the man who had organised Professor Christie's trip. Doctor Feng and his son would be meeting them at the landing-strip and taking them to the site itself.

Olly and Josh had become e-mail pals with Ang-Lun over the past couple of weeks. They were looking forward to meeting him at last and exchanging gifts. Ang-Lun was learning English, and from his e-mails he already seemed to be very fluent. Josh and Olly were bringing him a copy of *Treasure Island*, which he had told them was his favourite book, but which he had read only in Chinese so far.

The small plane continued its journey south along the shrunken course of the Minjiang, and it wasn't many minutes before Olly and Josh could clearly see the tall slopes of the sacred mountain looming on the horizon.

'We'll be landing soon,' Jonathan called. 'Seat-belts on, everyone.'

The plane lifted suddenly, soaring high up into the clear blue sky, leaving Olly's stomach somewhere far below. She and Josh had their noses pressed against the window as the mountain grew to fill the entire skyline, its upper reaches shrouded in mist and cloud. The pilot was climbing to fly over the mouth of the volcano. To the east, more mountains stretched away, rising and falling into the misty blue distance. Far, far off in that direction lay Tibet and Nepal and India. But Olly and Josh's attention was riveted on Si-Houzai-Shan.

The mountain was a broad rugged cone of grey-brown rock, treeless and raw in the slanting afternoon sunlight. The summit was a ring of broken peaks, several kilometres across, rising like daggers from the shreds of cloud that clung to the high slopes. The crater that lay within the broken crown of the mountain was filled with a dense blanket of white mist which veiled whatever lay beneath.

'The mountain is considered a sacred place by a lot of the local people,' Josh said.

'I can see why they'd think it was something special,' Olly replied, enchanted by the sight of the ancient volcano.

The plane skirted the mountain peak and began to circle downwards. Olly strained against her seat-belt, watching as the ground rose swiftly up to meet them. They had come to a place of brown baked earth, wrinkled and folded, and as dry as dust.

A flat stretch of land lay directly ahead. The world was rushing past now and the small aircraft was rattling and vibrating as the pilot throttled back and came in to land. There was a bump and a lurch as the wheels hit the ground. The plane rose again for a heart-stopping second, then came down with a thump. Olly and Josh were jolted in their seats as the plane came to a shuddering halt.

Olly grinned at Josh. 'Phew! That was exciting,' she said.

The next few minutes were spent getting everyone safely off the plane and piling the luggage by the side of the makeshift runway.

Olly looked around. There were a couple of dilapidated old buildings nearby, and a simple dirt road that snaked off among the hills – but there was no sign of life anywhere. 'I thought Doctor Feng was going to meet us,' she remarked. 'Where is he?'

'I'll find out,' Jonathan said. He tapped out a number on his mobile phone.

'We could do some exploring while we're waiting,' Olly suggested.

'No, stay put,' said her gran. 'I don't want you getting lost in the first five minutes.'

The professor shielded his eyes against the fierce sunlight as he scanned the horizon. 'Odd,' he said.

'We landed right on time, and Doctor Feng definitely said he'd be here to meet us. Perhaps he's running a little late.'

'I hope he comes soon,' Josh murmured. 'I don't fancy lugging our gear to the site on foot.' He looked at Jonathan. 'It's about two kilometres away, isn't it?'

Jonathan nodded, but he was frowning – obviously there was no answer to his call yet.

'I don't think it will come to that,' Audrey Beckmann said. 'Now then, would anyone like something to drink while we're waiting? I've got some bottles of mineral water around here somewhere.' She rummaged in one of her bags.

Olly wandered to a high point a little way off, where she could see further along the grey dirt-road. 'Someone's coming!' she called. A battered and dust-coated old Land Cruiser was making its way towards the landing strip.

Olly ran back to join the rest of the party as the vehicle came to a halt. A Chinese man stepped out. He looked to be in his forties. His clothes were dirt-encrusted and his hands and face were grimy. Olly guessed that he had come straight from the dig without having had time to clean up.

24

The professor greeted him with a smile. 'Doctor Feng,' he said. 'It's a pleasure to meet you again.'

But Olly saw that the doctor's face was troubled. 'I am sorry I am late,' he apologised. 'But there has been a terrible accident at the site. People have been injured. Professor Andryanova has been taken to hospital.' He looked around the stunned group. 'The local diggers are saying that the ruins are cursed, and many have abandoned the site,' he added. 'They say that if we continue to violate the sacred mountain, we will all die. It is a disaster.'

Olly and Josh stared at one another, their breath quite taken away by Doctor Feng's startling news. It seemed as if more than just a drought was afflicting the land that lay in the shadow of Si-Houzai-Shan – the dead fire mountain.

Chapter Two

The Curse

Olly's high spirits had taken a severe knock with Doctor Feng's news of the accident at the dig. The Christie party was subdued as the Land Cruiser took the last bend in the rough earth road, and they saw ahead of them the wide, sun-baked banks of the Minjiang River.

As Josh had shown Olly on an Internet map, the river made a wide loop around the sacred mountain, running through a wilderness of hills and valleys that grew ever more steep and rugged as they neared the foot of the mountain.

Si-Houzai-Shan utterly dominated the landscape. The late afternoon sun had dropped away behind it, throwing much of its mass into deep shade, but painting its outer contours with shining gold. The wisps and tatters of cloud that hung around its barren upper slopes glowed with an eerie, translucent light.

The four-by-four pulled into the camp at the archaeological dig site and came to a halt. Olly climbed out and stood staring up at the mountain's majestic bulk, feeling suddenly very small and insignificant beneath its long shadow. She could understand how people might believe the mountain was sacred – there was something about it that inspired awe.

'Don't just stand there gawping, Olivia,' snapped her gran. 'Help us unload.'

Olly tore her eyes away from the mountain as her gran pushed a heavy bag into her hands. She looked around, taking in the rest of her surroundings. The Land Cruiser was parked on the long gentle slope of the dry riverbank. The brown river trailed sluggishly through rocks and boulders ten or more metres away. Off to one side, Olly saw what they had come all this way to investigate – the broken walls and towers of an ancient town rose out of untold centuries of river silt and mud. In the other direction, a cluster of wooden huts and cabins had been constructed for the archaeologists to live in while they worked. A few dusty cars and trucks were parked behind the buildings, alongside three industrial digging machines. A section of the ruins had been cordoned off with red and white tape. That was obviously where the accident had occurred.

Before Doctor Feng's revelations, Olly had imagined that the place would be bustling with activity, but the small number of people who remained were standing or sitting in small, subdued groups. Some were obviously locals, dressed in simple tops and trousers of brown and tan and orange. Olly noticed that they were all quite young.

There was also a group of downcast field archaeologists who sat silently together, obviously badly affected by the accident. Some were Chinese, but Olly knew that the rest came from a variety of other countries – including Russia and America – and from Europe.

While they were still unloading their luggage, a man approached them from the huts. He looked Chinese, but he was not dressed for work on the site – he was wearing a grey tunic and trousers that

Olly thought had a somewhat military look about them. His eyes were hidden behind dark glasses. Two similarly-dressed men appeared and stood at his back – one of them Chinese, the other probably European or American.

'This is Charles Lau,' Doctor Feng told Professor Christie.

Lau shook the professor's hand unsmilingly. 'We've been expecting you, Professor,' he said in perfect, American-accented English. 'I hope you had a pleasant journey. I am Mr Bell's personal representative at this excavation. My job is to ensure that the work can progress and to prevent any potential problems between the people working on the dig and the locals.'

Olly looked at the dour-faced man, thinking that he seemed curiously out of place here. She didn't like the fact that his eyes were concealed behind dark glasses – it made him look as if he had something to hide.

'Why should there be any problems between us and the local people?' Jonathan asked.

Lau gave him a humourless smile. 'There shouldn't be,' he said. 'A few local people are angry that foreigners have been brought in to plunder their land, as they see it. They believe that they should benefit from whatever is found here. They do not understand that the work you are doing is for scientific purposes rather than profit. They are disorganised and ignorant farmers, that is all. They present no difficulty to my people – all of whom are highly-trained professionals. However, I recommend that you keep to this immediate area. I cannot guarantee the safety of anyone who wanders off alone.'

Olly didn't like the tone of disdain in Lau's voice as he spoke about the local people. And from the look on Josh's face, she could tell that he had also taken a strong dislike to Augustus Bell's 'personal representative'.

Audrey Beckmann stepped up to the man. 'Are you suggesting we might be in physical danger from the local people?' she asked.

'I lead an elite team,' said Lau. 'I can assure you that we will not allow you to be inconvenienced by a few trouble-makers.' He nodded briefly to Doctor Feng and to Professor Christie, then turned sharply on his heel and marched off towards the huts. His two men followed.

Jonathan frowned after them. 'What do you

make of that?' he said. 'They look like security guards to me. Why would Bell feel the need to hire men like that?'

'Unfortunately there is some local unrest,' Doctor Feng admitted. 'But don't be alarmed by Lau. The people who farm around here are poor, and they are suffering badly from the drought, but they are kindly and gentle – and I can assure you that they will do nothing to impede our work.'

'I hope you're right, Doctor,' Professor Christie said with a frown. He looked over towards the ruins. 'Before we do anything else, perhaps we should see how the accident happened,' he suggested.

Doctor Feng led Jonathan and the professor over towards the ruins. Olly and Josh followed them while Olly's gran bustled off to start unpacking.

The red and white tape surrounded the shell of a building. There were signs that some major digging had already taken place. Within the broken walls, a pit had been excavated, some four metres deep. To one side, a whole section of the ancient wall had clearly fallen in, strewing the ground with rubble and debris.

'The walls have not been properly shored-up,'

Olly heard her father murmur to himself as he examined the excavation. 'How very unsafe.' He shook his head. 'And this isn't the first time I've seen Andryanova cut corners.' He frowned and fell silent as he noticed an interesting carving and bent down to examine it more closely.

'Was anyone seriously hurt?' Olly asked, peering down into the deep trench.

'Professor Andryanova broke his leg,' Doctor Feng replied. 'Thankfully, the others only suffered cuts and bruises. The real problem is that most of the people we hired locally have deserted us. As you can see, only a few of the younger ones stayed behind, and if anything else goes wrong, I think we'll lose them too. It will take several days to bring in new workers from towns further away – if they will come at all, once news of the accident spreads.'

'Do you mean because of the curse?' Olly asked. 'Why *do* they think the place is cursed?'

Jonathan shook his head. 'That's not important right now,' he said. 'Our real problem is how to keep the dig running with so few workers.'

Professor Christie was a little way off, stooping to scrutinise a section of walling. Doctor Feng approached him. 'While Professor Andryanova is in hospital, would you be prepared to take over as the team-leader?' he asked.

Professor Christie looked around distractedly. 'Hmm?' He frowned. 'Oh, no, I don't think so. I'm here to investigate the ruins, not to run the dig,' he said. 'Is there no one else?'

'No one with your authority or expertise,' replied Doctor Feng.

'Someone needs to take control,' Jonathan pointed out to the professor. 'We have to put some health and safety precautions in place before anyone can work here.'

Professor Christie sighed. 'That's true,' he acknowledged. He straightened up, his forehead creased. 'Very well,' he said to Doctor Feng. 'I'll take *temporary* responsibility for the excavation.'

'It's getting late now,' Jonathan said. 'But first thing in the morning, I'll organise a team to begin work on making sure the site is safe.'

They all turned and headed back the way they had come. Olly walked alongside Josh. 'Great,' she said gloomily. 'We've come all this way, and now we can't do anything.' She frowned at her father and Doctor Feng, deep in conversation as they walked back towards the encampment of small wooden buildings. 'I know Jonathan said it wasn't important, but I'd really like to know why some of the local people think this place is cursed,' she added.

As they approached the cluster of buildings, a Chinese boy burst out from one of the cabins and ran towards them. He was wearing jeans and a T-shirt, his face wreathed in smiles.

'That's Ang-Lun!' Olly exclaimed, recognising him from an e-mailed exchange of photographs. She looked at Josh. 'Where's the present we brought for him?'

Josh took the hardback copy of *Treasure Island* from his bag.

'Hello Olly, hello Josh,' Ang-Lun said, grinning. 'I have very looked forward to meeting you. I have been helping to prepare food for everyone. I will show you where you will be sleeping.'

'This is for you,' Josh said, handing Ang-Lun the book. Olly noticed that Josh was careful to hold the book in both hands as he passed it to Ang-Lun, since Chinese people saw this as an especially respectful gesture.

Ang-Lun was clearly delighted by the gift and he

cradled it in his arms as they walked towards the buildings.

The Chinese boy explained that he and his father were staying at his grandmother's house in nearby Banping – a small village a kilometre or so to the north. He showed Olly and Josh to a two-roomed cabin. Josh and Jonathan were to sleep in the larger of the rooms, and Olly in the other. The professor and Audrey Beckmann were sharing an adjacent building. The rest of the archaeological team were staying in various other huts, which were gathered around a much larger cabin used for cooking and eating. There was another hut for washing and several more for storing equipment – one of which held a generator and barrels of fuel-oil to supply the site with power.

Lau and his men had their own quarters a little way off – according to Ang-Lun, they kept very much to themselves and even prepared and ate their food separately.

Having shown them around the campsite, Ang-Lun presented Josh and Olly with a rolled scroll. Olly unrolled it to see a coloured illustration, drawn on paper made from bamboo pulp. It showed a curious scene. A man in bright red traditional Chinese costume was standing on a hillside, his arms raised, his face astonished. Hovering in the air above him, her feet in clouds, was a woman. She was wearing traditional dress – her long silken ribbons fluttered in the wind – and she smiled serenely down at the man in red. The sky was dark blue, and behind the woman's head was the full moon.

'They are Chang-O and Hou-Yi,' Ang-Lun explained. 'Chang-O is about to fly off to the moon. My grandmother painted it for you when I told her that you were interested in the story.'

'It's wonderful,' Olly said, enchanted by the delicate picture. 'Please thank your grandmother for us.'

'You will be able to thank her yourselves at the festival,' Ang-Lun told them.

'What festival is that?' Josh asked.

Ang-Lun looked surprised. 'Didn't you know?' he replied. 'The Festival of the Autumn Moon will be taking place in Chung-Hsien in two days' time. It's a celebration of the moon goddess, Chang-O. There will be lion dances and dragon dances, music in the streets and people wearing traditional costume.' He grinned. 'And lots of mooncakes to eat. Then, at the end, there will be many fireworks. Chung-Hsien isn't far away. You must all come – it's great fun.'

'We wouldn't miss it,' Olly said, her eyes shining.

Josh looked thoughtfully at Ang-Lun. 'Mr Lau said we should keep away from the local people,' he said. 'He told us some of them don't like us being here – is that true?'

Ang-Lun's normally smiling face clouded. 'A few are unhappy that the old city has been found,' he explained. 'They believe that it is cursed. They think the ruins should be left alone, and that if we continue digging, the sky god will show his anger by refusing to let it rain ever again.'

'Why do they think the city is cursed?' asked Olly.

'They believe that the sky god made the river rise on purpose to cover the city,' Ang-Lun continued. 'The Shan-Ren said that it was to punish the people for making Chang-O welcome after she had stolen Hou-Yi's pill of everlasting life.' He shook his head. 'Some of the older people are very superstitious.'

'What's the Shan-Ren?' Olly asked.

Ang-Lun looked at her. 'The Shan-Ren were the

guardians of the sacred mountain,' he said. 'But they died out a long time ago.'

'You mean they were a kind of secret society?' Josh exclaimed.

Ang-Lun nodded. 'Some of the older people still believe in the Shan-Ren's teachings, but the younger people aren't really interested.' Ang-Lun smiled. 'And I don't believe in curses.'

'Don't be too sure about that,' Josh warned. 'Olly's family has a curse on it, by all accounts.'

Olly glared at him. 'Thanks for bringing that up,' she said. She turned to Ang-Lun, who was gazing at her in surprise. 'It's nothing, really,' she told him. 'An ancestor of mine took a scroll from an old tomb in Egypt. The scroll had a curse on it, that's all.' She shrugged and fell silent.

'Tell him the rest,' Josh urged. He looked at Ang-Lun. 'The curse said that the first-born son in each generation of the family would die young. So far, they all have – including Olly's Uncle Douglas, that's her father's older brother! In fact, that's one of the reasons why the professor is so interested in finding all the Talismans of the Moon. He thinks they'll lead him to the Hall of Records. Then he can get a copy of the scroll, put it back in the tomb and break the curse before anyone else dies,' he finished triumphantly.

Ang-Lun looked confused. 'I don't understand,' he said. 'What is the "Hall of Records"?'

'It's an ancient library,' Olly explained. 'No one knows where it is, but it's supposed to have copies of every sacred writing that was ever made back in ancient times.' She sighed, wishing Josh had never brought this up. 'Back in the last century, my Great-uncle Adam believed that if the scroll was taken back to the tomb, then the curse would be lifted. Unfortunately, Adam *and* the original scroll were both lost at sea when the ship he was on went down in a storm.' She narrowed her eyes thoughtfully. 'I don't think my dad really believes in the curse – but it was finding out about it that got him interested in archaeology in the first place.'

Ang-Lun looked at Olly. 'You told me you have no brothers,' he said to her. 'So, even if the curse was real, it can't do any more harm.'

Olly didn't reply. She didn't want to mention the dark thoughts that sometimes kept her awake at night. For three generations, the eldest-born of the Christie family had met a sudden and tragically early death. They had all been sons – but what if there were no sons for the curse to destroy?

What if there was only a daughter?

What if there was only Olly?

Chapter Three

The Ruined City

Josh slept soundly that night, worn out by the long journey and the change in time zones. A good sleep helped to adjust his body-clock a little, and the enticing smell of cooking that came in through the open window of his bedroom the following morning soon had him up and dressed.

Jonathan's bed was empty. Josh assumed he had risen early to get working on the site.

Yawning, Josh thumped on Olly's bedroom door. 'You up?' he called. Josh heard grumbling from within. Olly was not at her best first thing in the morning – especially when eight o'clock in the morning in Sechuan Province was one o'clock in the morning back home! 'Get up!' Josh called. 'You'll miss breakfast.'

He stepped down out of the cabin. The morning was fresh and clear. Above him, the sky was a lovely pale blue and cloudless. He could see activity over at the ruins – people were busy with long timbers and sheets of boarding. He could see Jonathan perched on a section of walling, wielding a hammer. The sound of the hammer blows drifted on the faint breeze.

A couple of Lau's men were standing nearby on a crest of high ground, watching the workers.

Josh hurried over to the dining cabin. Professor Christie and Doctor Feng were huddled together at a corner table, poring over documents and talking eagerly together in low voices. A young Chinese woman was at the griddle, tossing a thick, sweet-smelling pancake while Audrey Beckmann looked on.

'Hello, Josh,' Olly's gran said. 'Did you sleep well? Are you hungry?'

'Yes and yes,' Josh replied. 'I called Olly, but she just moaned at me.'

'I did not moan,' came Olly's voice from the doorway. 'I just don't like being yelled at.' She was dressed and bright-eyed. 'What's for brea

'Wei-Li is making us *jian bing*,' Audrey Beckm
said. 'It's a kind of crêpe. Go and sit down. I'll
bring the food over to you.'

Their first Chinese breakfast began with a bowl
of *mian cha* – thick, sweet porridge made from
millet. It was topped with sesame paste and
sprinkled with sesame seeds. Josh and Olly ate it
hungrily with broad china spoons, and drank fresh
milk from delicate porcelain cups.

Audrey Beckmann brought them the *jian bing*,
plump and browned from the frying pan. 'When
you've finished eating, you can come over to my
room for your lessons,' she said firmly.

Olly frowned at her. 'Do we have to?' she asked.
'I was hoping we could help Dad and Jonathan – it
is our first day, after all.'

'You've already missed two days of lessons,' her
gran reminded her. 'Besides, I don't think Jonathan
will want you anywhere near the site until he's
finished making sure everything is safe.' She gave
them a stern look. 'I want you both in my room
with your school books in half an hour, OK?'

Olly and Josh nodded. There was no point
arguing with her. Once Mrs Beckmann had made

even Olly's powers of persuasion
her mind. Besides, as Olly pointed
hile they finished their breakfast, once
over for the day, they would have the
he afternoon in which to explore.

By midday, when the two friends emerged from their makeshift schoolroom, the sun was burning down bright and hot, filling the air with fine red dust and causing distances to shimmer in a heat-haze.

The dining area was much busier than it had been at breakfast time. Jonathan was there, eating lunch along with a team of field archaeologists and eight or nine locals – young people who had returned to the site to work, either because they didn't believe in the curse or – as Jonathan pointed out to Olly and Josh – because they needed the money.

The two friends had a quick lunch of noodle soup, before checking with Jonathan that it was safe for them to go and explore the ruins.

'That's fine,' he told them. 'Just be sensible, and don't go near any of the areas I've taped off. You might want to go and check out the finds hut, too – there's some interesting stuff in there.'

This sounded like a good idea, so before they went exploring, they took a detour to the cabin where everything found on the dig was gathered for cleaning and cataloguing.

It was an extraordinary collection. There were countless shards of earthenware, but much more interesting were the golden cups and plates and bowls. Most of them were damaged, eroded and distorted from centuries under the ground – but some looked as bright and perfect as when they had first been made. There were exquisite statuettes of green jade and figurines of bronze and ivory. A young archaeologist called Nadia, speaking in English with a thick Russian accent, explained that the artefacts dated back nearly three-and-a-half thousand years.

Made even more eager to explore by what they had seen, Josh and Olly headed for the ruins. From what Josh could make out as they approached, about a quarter of the area had been made safe so far. The rest was still taped off.

They stepped down into the first of the long trenches and, with a real sense of wonder, entered the dead city. In some places the only trace of the building that had once stood there was a single row of stonework or a section of flooring. But elsewhere, entire stone walls towered over Josh and Olly's heads – cracked, broken and discoloured from centuries under the rushing waters of the Minjiang, but solid and impressive nevertheless. Here and there, they were able to enter rooms or corridors, and walk on newly-excavated floors where no one had set foot since the river had risen in ancient times.

They saw the results of the team's work so far. In some of the rooms, there were semi-revealed finds – the mouth of an earthenware jar sunk into the ground, for example, or a barely-recognisable piece of ivory protruding from the dry mud and tagged for careful, painstaking removal, once the site had been made safe to Professor Christie's exacting standards.

Olly stood in the middle of a large room with high stone walls. 'I can see why some people might think this place is cursed,' she remarked to Josh. 'It's a bit creepy – and it's so cold.'

Josh had also noticed the strange chill that lingered in the ruined buildings – a coldness that seemed to seep from the stones and flow through the rooms and corridors despite the intense heat of the sun.

He scrambled up a chunk of time-worn masonry, and stared out towards the mountain, shading his eyes from the sun. 'If this really was a city, where's the rest of it?' he called down to Olly. 'All the buildings they've found so far wouldn't really make a decent-sized town.' He spotted a solitary stone building a few hundred metres away amongst the hills. 'I wonder what that is?' he said, pointing. It was on higher ground than the ruins, and although it was obviously old and partly-ruined, it didn't have the same battered and worn look as the old city.

There was no reply from Olly. Josh looked down and saw that she had wandered off. 'Keep away from the taped-off areas,' he called.

'I will,' came Olly's reply.

Josh continued to explore on his own, making his way gradually towards the stone building in the hills. He climbed down into a long trench with freshly-dug stonework in the sides and floor. He moved slowly, peering intently down and around, hoping to spy some tell-tale colour or shape that would turn out to be a previously-missed but priceless artefact. He smiled to himself, thinking how envious Olly would be if he found something amazing.

Suddenly, he realised that he was now close to the strange, solitary building he had been heading for, *and* that he was near to the place where the accident had happened. He climbed out of the trench and stared down into the pit where Andryanova and his team had been working when the wall collapsed. A scaffolding of timber framed the walls now.

Josh noticed that a similar pit had been excavated alongside. It was surrounded by a waist-high wall, broken and decaying and about half a metre thick. The excavation was still taped off. Josh leant over the wall and found himself peering down into a sunken chamber. He guessed the drop was about six metres on to a floor of silt and crumbling earth.

He was about to draw back and go in search of Olly when a glint of something caught his eye. It was in the wall of the room – only half a metre below where he was standing. He leant further over, trying to make sense of what he was seeing.

It was about the size of his hand and it was set back in the wall. It had only been revealed because a great chunk seemed to have recently fallen away. There was no tag to show that the artefact had been spotted by anyone else, and it struck Josh that perhaps the collapse of the other wall had caused vibrations which made the mud fall away. If that was the case, then he was the first person to see this thing for thousands of years!

He hesitated for a moment. Perhaps he should go and tell Jonathan about it – that would probably be the sensible thing to do, he thought. On the other hand, if he leant just a little bit further over, it would be within arm's reach. It would be quite something to just stroll up to Jonathan and the professor and hand them a brand new artefact! Olly would be green with envy – she was usually the one to do impetuous things like that.

Josh couldn't resist trying. He leant further over, lying across the broken top of the wall and reaching down as far as he could. His fingertips were only centimetres away from the shining object. As he touched it, another piece of its mud coating fell away, revealing more of the object. Josh stared breathlessly down at it. He could now see a half-circle of gold embedded in the mud – and he was sure there were some kind of markings on it.

He strained to reach down those last few maddening millimetres. His fingers scrabbled at the object, and more earth broke away. He lifted his feet off the ground, squirming forwards on the broad top of the wall. Now his fingertips could actually touch the cold metal. He grinned – almost there!

And then, as he stretched downwards to get a grip on the object, he slipped forwards. For a horrible moment he hung there, knowing he was going to fall but unable to pull himself back. Then the balance tipped, and with a loud yell, Josh toppled head first into the chamber below.

Chapter Four

Missing!

Josh twisted as he fell, landing heavily on one shoulder and rolling on the soft earth. He lay gasping for breath and grimacing in pain for a few moments. Then, having decided he wasn't badly hurt, he opened his eyes and stared round at the walls of the chamber. They were smooth and featureless and there were no window holes. There was a doorway, but the door itself had long since decayed away, and the exit was blocked by a solid wall of packed earth.

'Nice going, Josh,' he groaned to himself. 'That's the last time you behave like Olly!' He looked down at his clothes. '*And* it's the last time you wear a white shirt on a dig!' he added. And then he realised that there was something cold and smooth under his right hand. He sat up, ignoring the aches and pains, and picked the thing up. It was a golden disc, about twenty centimetres across. Somehow he had managed to snatch it out of the wall as he had plunged past.

He grinned, forgetting his problems for a moment as he studied the beautiful artefact. He had been right about the markings – a series of little dimpled depressions had been punched into the surface of the golden disc – and from what Josh could make out, they formed a street plan of a large city.

'What are you doing down there?'

Josh looked up, startled by the voice from above. Olly's head and shoulders were dark against the sky as she leant out over the top of the wall.

'I slipped,' Josh responded. He got to his feet and lifted the golden disc up towards her. 'But look what I found.'

'What is it?'

'I don't know,' Josh said. 'But I'm pretty sure it's made of gold.'

'Wow!' Olly breathed. 'Come on up so I can have a proper look at it.'

Josh blinked up at her. 'How?' he asked.

She frowned and looked at the walls below. 'Can't you climb out?' she asked after a moment.

Josh shaded his eyes against the bright sky. 'Could *you*?' he demanded pointedly.

'I wouldn't have fallen down there in the first place,' Olly retorted. 'You are an idiot, Josh. I'm going to have to go and get help. And then Jonathan and Dad will skin us alive – this place is still taped off.'

'I know,' Josh said ruefully. 'I didn't fall down here on purpose. Can't you just get a rope or something without telling anyone?' It occurred to Josh that finding the golden disc would not be a good enough excuse for putting himself in danger. He didn't like to think about what Mrs Beckmann would have to say.

'I'll see what I can do,' Olly replied. She disappeared for a moment, then her head popped back over the wall. 'Don't go away,' she added with a grin.

'Oh, ha, ha,' Josh called up. 'Just get on with it, please, before someone comes.'

Olly vanished again and Josh sat down cross-legged on the ground. He held the golden disc in his hands and leant over it, studying the intricate markings – waiting to be rescued.

Olly ran through the ruins back towards the camp. She needed to rescue Josh quickly before the others finished their lunch and headed back to the site. She smiled to herself – it was unusual for Josh to get himself into trouble like this. Nine times out of ten, it would have been Olly down the hole, and Josh would have had to rescue *her*.

She felt a little envious that he had found the golden disc – but she was more intrigued than anything else. She couldn't wait to get Josh out and have a good look at it.

She headed for the equipment huts. There was bound to be rope in there somewhere. She glanced over at the dining cabin, fearing she'd see the team coming out to get back to work. But the door was closed and there was no sign of anyone. She found a coil of thick rope, slung it over her shoulder and ran towards the ruins.

'I'm back,' she called. 'I'm just going to tie one end on to something, then I'll let the rope down.' Her mouth curled in a wry smile. 'I suppose you know how to climb a rope?' she added.

There was no reply.

She frowned. 'I was only kidding,' she called, assuming Josh hadn't been impressed by her joke.

Still nothing.

She peered over the wall. 'Oh!' She stared down into the sunken room, hardly able to believe her eyes. Josh was gone.

She assumed he must have managed to climb out on his own, so she stood upright, and looked around. 'Josh?' she called.

But he was nowhere to be seen.

She shouted, 'Jo-osh!'

Nothing.

Olly's eyes narrowed. It was dawning on her that Josh had only *pretended* he couldn't climb out. 'I know what he's done,' she muttered to herself. 'He's taken that golden thingy to show to Dad without me.' She snorted. 'I bet he doesn't mention how he found it!'

Forgetting the rope, she trudged, irritated, back to the camp. As she arrived, she saw Jonathan's team leaving the dining cabin. 'Where is he?' she asked Jonathan. 'Is he in there with Dad?'

Jonathan gave her a puzzled look. 'Do you mean Josh?'

'Of course I mean Josh,' she said. 'I suppose he's been showing off with that thing.'

'What thing?' Jonathan asked. 'What are you talking about, Olly? I haven't seen Josh since the two of you went off together half an hour ago.'

'Oh.' Olly stared at him in surprise. 'I thought . . .' She frowned. 'Is Dad still in there?'

'Yes, he's talking with Doctor Feng and Mr Lau,' Jonathan replied.

'And you haven't seen Josh at all?' Olly queried.

Jonathan looked suspiciously at her. 'What have you two been up to?' he demanded. 'Has he wandered off somewhere?'

'No,' Olly answered quickly. 'We were just exploring the ruins, and I kind of lost track of him.'

'What's this *thing* you were talking about?' Jonathan asked.

'He found something,' Olly replied. 'I thought he'd come here to show it to you and Dad.'

'No, he didn't,' Jonathan said, still regarding Olly dubiously.

Olly decided it was time to go before Jonathan asked any more awkward questions. 'Perhaps he went back to the cabin,' she said. 'I'll just go and check.' She ran over to their cabin, a small knot of anxiety forming in her stomach. Where on earth had Josh got to?

She pushed the door to Josh and Jonathan's room open. Josh wasn't there. 'OK,' Olly said to herself. 'This is getting silly. He has to be somewhere.'

She ran over to the hut with the washrooms – still no sign of him. Really worried now, she ran from hut to hut, but Josh was nowhere to be found. Olly thought that it was as if he had just vanished off the face of the Earth.

'What's going on?' Audrey Beckmann's voice brought Olly to a halt. 'Jonathan tells me that Josh has disappeared.'

Olly was now too concerned about Josh to bother hiding the truth. 'He fell into a big hole,' she said, waving an arm towards the ruins. 'I went to get some rope to haul him out, but when I got back, he was gone!'

'Come and show me where you mean,' Mrs Beckmann said.

By this time, Jonathan had explained the situation to Professor Christie. So Olly led the professor, Doctor Feng, her gran and Jonathan over to the ruins. Mr Lau followed silently behind them.

'He was down there,' Olly said, pointing into the sunken room.

Jonathan stared down into the pit. 'He shouldn't have been anywhere near here,' he said. 'What did I tell you about taking care?'

'I know,' Olly said miserably. 'But he saw something sticking out of the wall – and when he leant over to try and get it . . .' She didn't need to finish the sentence.

Lau stepped forwards and stared into the room below. 'What did the boy find?' he asked Olly.

She looked at him. 'It was some kind of golden disc,' she said, holding her hands apart, 'about this big.'

Lau took out a radio and spoke rapidly into it in Mandarin. Then he turned to the professor. 'I don't think the boy can have climbed out on his own,' he said. 'The walls are too smooth. Someone else must have been here. I'll have my men begin a search.' He turned to Olly. 'How long ago did this happen?'

'Only a few minutes,' Olly replied.

'Good, then they won't have got far – unless they have some kind of transport. Let's hope that's not the case.'

'Mr Lau,' Audrey Beckmann broke in. 'I'd be very grateful if you'd explain what you mean.'

Lau turned to face her, his eyes, as ever, hidden behind his dark glasses. 'I think the boy has been kidnapped,' he said flatly. 'Possibly, they only wanted the golden disc, but they may intend to hold him for ransom. This is the first time any outsider has dared to come on site. It certainly won't happen again.' He stalked off, talking rapidly into his radio.

'We should search, too,' Jonathan said. 'I'll organise everyone into groups. With any luck Lau's wrong, and we'll find Josh somewhere nearby.'

'I'll help,' Olly said.

'No, you won't,' her gran contradicted. 'You'll go straight back to your cabin and stay there.'

'But . . .'

'Do as you're told, Olivia,' said her father.

Frustrated, annoyed and very worried for Josh, Olly made her way miserably back to the huts. Could Lau really be right? Had Josh been kidnapped? It didn't seem possible – but what other explanation could there be for his strange and sudden disappearance?

* * *

Half the afternoon had gone past and Olly was climbing the walls in frustration. She ran from window to window in the cabin in the hope of seeing someone coming back with Josh. She could see people in the distance – search parties ranging the hills. She chewed a nail, wishing she could be out there with them. The uncertainty and inactivity was driving her crazy.

She saw Jonathan approaching and leant out of the window. 'Any sign of Josh?' she asked, already guessing the answer from his face. He looked tired and anxious.

'Nothing so far,' Jonathan replied.

Olly looked at him, trying not to sound as frightened for Josh as she felt. 'Perhaps Doctor Feng was right – and this place really is cursed.'

'Don't be silly, Olly,' Jonathan said, frowning at her. 'It's more likely that Lau is right and Josh has been kidnapped.' He set his jaw. 'Your gran has called the police in Chung-Hsien. They should arrive soon. In the meantime, all we can do is keep searching.' He looked up at her. 'You've got your mobile phone, haven't you? So you can call me if he turns up.'

Olly nodded.

Jonathan turned and set off up the long dry riverbank at a steady jog.

Olly sank down on one of the beds. Sitting around and waiting for news went against every instinct in her body. She wanted to be out there. She wanted to find Josh.

For a long moment, she gazed out of the window, her eyes ranging over the hills, her fingers rattling impatiently on the window sill while she thought through the options – wait here or go and help.

Eventually she got to her feet, her mind made up – waiting was impossible. She ran across the room and slipped out of the door. She would be very careful – and if she saw anything suspicious, she had her mobile phone to call for help. She decided to search for some clues back at the sunken room where she had last seen Josh. The search parties were ranging further out into the countryside now, and the ruins were deserted.

Fortunately, the coil of rope was still lying where she had dropped it. She quickly looped the rope around a jutting chunk of masonry and knotted it. She let it out into the room and climbed down.

The first thing that struck her was how chilly it was down amongst the ruins. The day was so hot and humid that the cold took her by surprise. She shivered as she looked at the walls. The ancient stonework was smooth and precise – the joints between the big blocks of stone would not even allow for a finger to be inserted. There was no way Josh could have climbed out – not unless someone else had helped him.

She crouched to examine the floor. The ground was soft in places. She could see the print of Josh's shoes quite clearly, here and there. But in other places the earth was sun-baked and hard. The sun was sinking now in the western sky, throwing long cold shadows across the room.

Something glinted by the wall on the other side of the room, catching her eye. She walked over to it and picked it up, turning it over in her fingers. It was a white shirt button – quite clean and new. She frowned. Josh had been wearing a white shirt. She looked up at the wall next to the button. The stonework was as sheer as it was on all the other walls. She was sure Josh couldn't have climbed up here either.

But then she noticed a crevice in the rock at shoulder height. She leant forwards and peered into the hole. All she saw was blackness. She took her small pencil-torch out of her pocket, and switching it on, shone the powerful, thin white beam into the hole. Still she could see nothing. The torchlight illuminated the sides of the hole, but did not reveal how deep it was.

Olly pushed her forefinger into the hole, and felt something very cold and smooth against her fingertip. It wasn't stone, she was sure. It felt more like metal.

She pressed her fingers against the metal thing and heard a soft, sharp click. The wall moved slightly and she snatched her hand away in surprise. A section of the wall, about two metres high and one metre wide, had moved smoothly inwards.

Cautiously, she pushed this section of the stone wall with one hand. It gave, swinging open silently to reveal a deep dark space from which a cold, clammy air flowed. She pointed her torch into the darkness. It illuminated some kind of small, dusty room.

'Josh?' Olly called tentatively. 'Josh – are you in there?' She stepped forwards nervously, her mouth dry, her stomach knotting. 'Josh?' she called again, stepping in through the stone doorway.

As she crossed the threshold, she caught a

movement out of the corner of her eye. A figure was lurking in the shadows to one side of the door. Before she had time to react, the figure lunged forwards, knocked the torch out of her hand and pulled her into the room. Olly stumbled and fell to the ground. And the stone doorway swung silently closed behind her, shutting out the light.

Chapter Five

Imprisoned

A voice spoke sharply in Olly's ear – words of warning or command in Mandarin. She scrambled towards her torch, which was lying on the floor, its beam lighting up a section of one wall.

A bright light flashed in her face. She lifted an arm to shield her eyes. 'Stop that!' she snapped.

The torch was angled away and more Mandarin was spoken. Olly got to her feet and backed against the wall, staring at the man in front of her. He was tall and wiry, and the lower half of his face was hidden behind a red silk scarf. Deep-shadowed eyes stared unblinkingly at her from beneath a leathery, lined forehead. Olly guessed that the man must be in his forties, at least. He was wearing the simple tunic and trousers of the local farmers.

He watched her with his deep, intent eyes. She licked her dry lips, wondering how she could escape. She stooped and picked up her torch. Then she circled the room, keeping her back to the wall. The man tracked her with the beam of his own torch.

Olly lunged for the doorway and struggled to get some kind of grip on the stonework, but like everything else it was smooth and featureless. She turned and looked back at the man, noticing as she did so that there was a black pictogram on the scarf that masked his face.

'I am Olivia Christie,' she said firmly, trying to sound as if she had everything under control. 'I want you to let me out of here right now.' She racked her brains for something to say in Mandarin. '*Qing!*' she said. Please.

The man spoke again.

'*Wo bu dong,*' Olly said, remembering more of the words her gran had taught her. '*Ni hui jiang yingyu ma?*' I don't understand – do you speak English?

The man nodded his head. He had understood her. That was something.

'OK,' Olly said slowly. 'I know how to say hello, goodbye, please and thank you, but I'm not sure any of that is going to help much.' She pointed to the door, making a gesture that she hoped he would understand meant she wanted to get out.

Again he shook his head, this time aiming his torch towards an open doorway in the far side of the room. He nodded towards her and pointed at the exit.

Olly was beginning to recover from her initial fright. The man didn't seem to mean her any immediate harm. His voice was quiet and calm and his behaviour was not especially threatening. 'You want me to go that way?' she asked, also pointing.

He nodded.

She looked at him. 'I don't suppose I have much choice, do I?' She sighed. Then she frowned. 'Who are you? What are you doing down here?'

The man spoke sharply, gesturing for her to move. She pocketed her torch and walked towards the far doorway, glancing over her shoulder to see him following close behind.

The doorway led into a narrow corridor. Occasionally, another doorway led off to one side or the other, but the man put a hand on Olly's shoulder, keeping her to the main passage.

Olly remembered the mobile phone that she had in her pocket. That made her feel better. As soon as she got the chance, she would try and call in a rescue party.

She looked around at the man. 'You've got Josh, too, haven't you?' she said. What was the Mandarin word for boy? '*Nanhair?*' she said. 'Boy? Are you taking me to Josh?' She frowned. 'Well, I hope you are. And when we get out of here, you're going to be in real big trouble, Mister – and that's a promise.'

The silent man pressed his hand down on Olly's shoulder, bringing her to a halt. She looked around. The corridor stretched on ahead of them and there was no obvious doorway nearby. Then the man reached into a square cavity in the wall and a section of it slid away to reveal a block of darkness.

Assuming this was their way forward, Olly moved towards the opening. But the man stopped her with one hand, and patted her pockets with the other. He found the bulge of her mobile phone and took it out.

'Here, wait a minute,' Olly said. 'You can't do that.'

But the man simply stepped aside and gave Olly a firm shove in the small of her back. She stumbled forwards into the darkness. The doorway slid closed at her back and the torchlight was cut off.

Olly turned and hammered on the cold stone. 'Hey! Let me out!' she shouted.

'I shouldn't bother,' came a weary voice out of the darkness. 'I tried that. He won't come back.'

Olly spun round. 'Josh?' she gasped. She fished in her pocket for the torch. At least the strange masked man had left her with that.

She switched it on. Josh was sitting in a corner of the small stone room. He lifted both hands to cover his eyes. 'Ow!' he said. 'Too bright!'

'Sorry.' She moved the light away, shining the beam around the room. It was windowless and doorless – a sealed stone box no more than four metres square.

Josh stood up and squinted at her.

'Are you OK?' she asked.

'Oh, fine,' Josh said dully. 'I'm having a great time. How long have I been here?'

'Several hours,' Olly told him. 'What happened?'

'I was grabbed from behind by two men and dragged through a doorway in the wall. They brought me here and then left.' He gestured to a chunk of bread and a bottle of water. 'They left me something to eat and drink,' he said. 'But they took the gold disc. I think that was what they really wanted.'

'Did they have scarves over their faces?' Olly asked.

Josh nodded.

Olly crouched and used her finger to draw the pictogram she had seen on the man's scarf in the dust that covered the stone floor. It was a simple symbol – like a capital E lying on its back, with the central stroke elongated, and an inverted Y over the top.

Josh squatted at her side. 'I saw that, too,' he said. They looked at one another. 'Do you know what it means?' he asked.

Olly shook her head. 'Mr Lau thinks you were kidnapped by criminals,' she remarked. 'I suppose it could be some kind of gang marking.' She stood up and walked over to the featureless section of masonry which hid the secret doorway. 'But whoever they are, we have to get out of here,' she said firmly. She ran the torchbeam over the wall, hoping to spot some hole or fissure that might contain another opening mechanism.

Josh joined her, and together they scoured the walls with eyes and hands.

'What do you think they're going to do with us?' Josh asked as they finished examining the walls.

'I don't plan on hanging around to find out,' Olly muttered. She aimed the torch upwards. The low ceiling was also made of stone blocks.

'We might be able to smash our way out if we can find something heavy to hit the wall with,' Josh suggested. He pointed to the corner of the room where a large stone slab lay on the floor. 'That might make a good battering-ram.'

Olly rested the torch on the floor and they both stooped to try and lift the stone. It was impossible for them to get their fingers under it, so they tried shifting it out of the corner, heaving and dragging with all their strength.

The stone moved a few centimetres. Josh got behind it and pushed with all his might. It moved again with the harsh grating noise of stone on stone. Josh suddenly found himself staring down at a black hole in the floor big enough to swallow him whole. He let out a startled yelp and jumped back into the corner.

An odd sound echoed up from the depths. A rushing, chattering, roaring sound – familiar but misplaced.

Olly knelt down and pointed her torch into the hole. It was a stone shaft – possibly two or three metres deep, and at the bottom, rippling and glinting in the torchlight, was a stream of flowing black water. 'It's some kind of well,' Olly announced. 'This water must run into the river, I suppose.'

'It does!' Josh agreed with sudden excitement. 'I saw it on the plan.'

Olly stared at him. 'What plan?'

'I forgot to tell you – there was a design punched out on the gold disc. It was a street-plan of a city. I think it was *this* city – Yueliang-Chengshi. It showed a waterway running through the city and down to the river.' He pointed at the rushing water below. 'This might be it.'

Olly looked thoughtfully at him. 'Which means that water down there is heading straight for the river, right?'

Josh nodded. 'We could throw something in – a

message to tell people where we are. It would end up in the river and someone would see it.' His eyes lit up. 'We'd be rescued.'

Olly looked at him. 'Except that we don't have anything to write on or anything to write with – or anything to put a message in so it wouldn't get wet.' She raised a single eyebrow. 'Apart from that – great plan.'

Josh sighed. 'You're right,' he said. 'It doesn't help us at all.'

'Unless we jump in, of course,' Olly suggested.

Josh gave a bleak laugh. 'Yes,' he said. 'We could always do that.'

'No. I mean it,' Olly insisted.

Josh looked at her. 'You want us to jump down the well?' he asked incredulously. 'Then what?'

'We swim,' Olly replied calmly, as if she was just suggesting a stroll over the hills.

'And what if there's no air?' Josh asked.

'We hold our breath,' Olly responded. She shone her torch down into the hole again. 'Look how fast the stream's going,' she said. 'We know the river isn't far away, so it can't run underground for long. We'll probably only have to hold our breath for a few seconds.' She looked at Josh. 'Unless you can think of another way to get us out of here – bearing in mind that this stone slab is too heavy for us to even pick up, never mind use as a battering-ram.'

Josh shook his head dubiously. 'How long can you hold your breath?' he asked.

'Long enough,' said Olly.

'You're not the greatest swimmer in the world, Olly,' he pointed out.

Olly frowned at him. 'And you are, I suppose?'

'I'm not saying that. I just think it's crazy to jump into the water without any idea of what's down there. We could both end up getting drowned.'

'Or we could sit here doing nothing till we're just a bunch of old bones,' Olly argued. 'Except that I'm not going to wait for that to happen. I don't care what you think – I'm going to give it a try.'

Josh looked thoughtfully at her for a few moments. 'Maybe we could do it,' he said. 'But you need to learn how to hold your breath properly underwater first.'

Olly sighed. 'I know how to hold my breath,' she said.

'Look, I can swim a full length of the swimming pool underwater,' Josh pointed out. 'What about you?'

'I don't know.'

'Exactly. The thing is, we only breathe with the top two-thirds of our lungs. So, you have to pant really fast before you take a big breath – that way all the carbon dioxide that's lying around in the bottom of your lungs gets stirred up and comes out, which leaves more room for oxygen.'

Olly stared at him. 'You know the weirdest things, Josh,' she said. 'Will the torch survive underwater?'

'It's supposed to be waterproof,' Josh replied. 'Now, do the panting thing,' he instructed. 'Then take a big breath and I'll time you to see how long you can hold it.'

Olly breathed in and out rapidly for a few seconds, then took a big gulp of air. Josh looked at his watch. Olly began to feel a tightness in her chest. It grew until she couldn't stand it any more. She forced herself to hold on for a few seconds longer, and then she let out the breath and gasped in some fresh air.

'That was only forty seconds,' Josh told her. He looked anxious. 'That's not very long. Maybe you should practise panting some more.'

Olly rolled her eyes and breathed in and out quickly for a few seconds, before taking another big gulp of air. Then, ignoring the look of surprise and dismay on Josh's face, she slid her legs over the edge of the well and pushed off with both hands.

Olly shut her eyes as she hit the water. It closed over her head, wrapping her in an icy darkness and filling her ears with the clamour of its rushing. Her feet touched the bottom with a shock which jarred through her. The torch fell out of her fingers and she felt herself being buffeted by the fast-flowing water. After the initial shock, it wasn't as cold as she had feared, but it was far stronger than she had anticipated. She floundered blindly and felt the bottom under her feet again.

She pushed up, thrusting her arms forwards, then forcing them back in a swimming motion. She felt herself moving along with the flow of water and felt a sense of relief. It was going to be OK – despite losing the torch, she knew she could do this. The tightness was beginning to grow in her chest, but not so fast that it worried her.

Her confidence was short-lived. She hit the wall of the tunnel hard with one shoulder. Bubbles of air escaped her lips, and grimacing with the pain of the impact, she tried to writhe clear of the wall.

But the current caught hold of her and twisted her round and round.

It was several moments before Olly managed to regain control of her body. Then she felt the bottom with her hands and feet again and felt some kind of debris gathered in the base of the channel. She realised she had to get clear – she couldn't risk getting snagged underwater – so she flexed her legs and pushed up hard – too hard. Her head struck the roof of the channel. The blood sang in her ears and, completely disorientated by the blow, she was tossed and turned in the torrent.

The pain grew in her lungs. Olly realised she had no idea which way up she was. She floundered, beginning to panic. Then she felt something catch her foot. She struggled to free herself, but there was something tangled around her shoe and she couldn't pull herself away. Red lights exploded in her eyes. The pain in her chest grew more intense. And Olly realised, in a horrible moment of clarity, that she wouldn't get to the surface in time – she was going to drown.

Chapter Six

Deep Water

'Olly!' Josh snatched at her clothes as she dropped down into the well, but it was too late. The last thing he saw before he was enveloped in darkness was Olly's figure entering the water with a loud splash. A moment later, the torchlight went out.

'Olly!' Cold water flew up the well, spattering Josh's face. He had to follow her – there was no choice. But he forced himself to count slowly to five before he moved. He didn't want to risk crashing down on top of her. It was dangerous enough, without that happening.

'I'm coming!' he called. He sat on the edge of the well, filled his lungs with air and dropped down.

The water was a shock, but Josh kept his head. His feet struck the bottom and he guessed the depth of the channel wasn't much more than his own height. He pushed off carefully, allowing himself to be carried by the powerful current, but also wary of hitting his head as he rose. He reached up blindly and felt smooth masonry-work against his groping fingers. Then in spite of his caution, his back struck the roof so that the breath was almost knocked out of his lungs.

Josh struck out, swimming strongly, feeling the curved roof of the channel scraping against his back and heels. He expected at any moment to feel Olly's feet or legs in front of him. He forged ahead, carried by the current, staring blindly into the swirling black water and hoping desperately to reach air before his lungs gave out.

And then, suddenly, the water was full of brightness. Josh pushed upwards and emerged into daylight. He gasped, treading water, flicking his head to get the hair out of his eyes as he looked around for Olly.

He had surfaced in a deep channel about six metres wide with high earth banks. Olly wasn't there.

His heart hammering, Josh took a huge breath and plunged back down, turning underwater and swimming back the way he had come. He guessed that Olly must still be down in the channel and he forced himself not to panic. There was still a chance. He estimated that he had not been under the water for much more than half a minute.

But Josh now had to fight against the powerful current. He forced his way deeper into the black tunnel, his eyes straining against the darkness, his hands feeling desperately for Olly.

His groping fingers brushed against something. It was Olly's arm. Josh turned, bracing his feet against the bottom of the channel and leaning back into the current. He tugged at the arm and for a dreadful moment, he thought he would not be able to pull Olly free. But then with a rush they were tumbling through the water. He kept a tight hold of his friend as he headed for light and air, determined that he wasn't going to lose track of her again.

They burst out of the water. Olly coughed and choked as Josh helped her to the bank. Together, they crawled up the slope and lay panting, side by side on the mud.

It was several seconds before Olly was able to speak. 'Piece of cake,' she gasped at last. She turned her head and smiled at Josh. 'What did I tell you?'

'What happened?' Josh asked.

'My foot got caught in something down there,' Olly replied. She frowned. 'It was getting pretty nasty.'

Josh sat up, and pushed wet hair off his face. 'I suppose I saved your life, then,' he commented.

Olly grinned and punched his arm. 'My hero,' she said. She stood up, her legs shaking, and looked around. 'Where are we?'

Josh followed her gaze. The channel came out from underneath a big, half-ruined stone building. He recognised it as the solitary old building he had seen from the ruins earlier that afternoon. He stood up. 'We'd better get back to camp,' he said. 'It's this way.'

Olly nodded, and they helped each other up the long slope to ground level.

Climbing to a high point, they saw that they were at the southern end of the ruins. The channel that had been their means of escape ran in a straight line under the solitary building and on into the river. They couldn't see where the water was coming from, but they assumed it must flow from the mountain.

Josh shivered as they walked back to the cabins. The sun was going down behind the mountain and his wet clothes were cold and heavy on his body.

As they neared the huts, they saw a door open. Olly's gran stood on the threshold. She stared for a moment, then shouted and began to run towards them. She took out a mobile phone and spoke into it as she ran – Josh guessed that she was giving out the good news.

Audrey Beckmann came to a halt in front of them, her face filled with relief.

'Hello, Gran,' Olly said with a tired grin. 'Look who I found! Someone had locked him up in a cellar back there.' She gestured towards the building. 'We had to swim through an underground passage to get out.'

Audrey Beckmann looked from one to the other, momentarily speechless. Her expression of relief changed to one of concern as she studied Josh. 'Are you all right, Josh?' she asked him.

'I'm fine,' he said. 'They didn't do anything to me.' He frowned. 'Except for swiping the gold disc I found.'

'That's the least of our worries right now,' Audrey Beckmann replied. 'Come with me and we'll get you cleaned up and into some dry clothes. The police will be here soon, so you can tell the full story then. And in the circumstances, Olly, I'll ignore the fact that you were told very clearly to stay in the camp.'

As they walked to the huts, Audrey Beckmann put her arms round their shoulders. 'I was so worried about you,' she said, hugging one and then the other. 'I'm glad you're both safe.'

Olly and Josh looked at one another. She wasn't the only one.

It was early evening. Olly and Josh were in the dining cabin, working their way through large bowls of spicy *kung pao* chicken. The professor was with them at the table, along with Jonathan, Olly's gran and Doctor Feng. The police officers from Chung-Hsien had recently departed, having taken statements from the two friends with Doctor Feng acting as translator.

Olly and Josh had taken them to the sunken room from which Josh had been abducted. Jonathan and the police officers had gone down into the hole, but in spite of Olly's instructions on how to open the hidden door, they had been unable to get the mechanism to work. Finally, they had allowed Olly down to demonstrate, but to her surprise and frustration, she found that the small metal tag within the hole was missing. She supposed that one of the mysterious masked men must have come back and removed it.

The police had insisted that the wall be broken down, so Professor Christie had given instructions for Jonathan and two members of the archaeological team to carefully take the wall apart. The professor had looked on, wincing as the stones were lifted out one by one. Olly knew that, under normal circumstances, the area would have been painstakingly excavated over several days, or even left entirely intact.

Finally, the room beyond the wall had been revealed. A brief exploration of the tunnels and other rooms had turned up no clues about Josh and Olly's captors. The rooms were empty, or more often, collapsed in on themselves. The tunnel that led to the old building where Olly and Josh had been imprisoned petered out in ever-larger rock-falls.

In their prison room itself, there was nothing – except for the remains of the bread and water left for Josh – to show that anyone had been down there for centuries.

Olly had drawn the pictogram she had seen on the men's scarves to show the police officers. She had got the impression that one of the men had recognised the symbol – but he had shaken his head and said nothing. Then supper had arrived and the police officers had gone.

As she ate her food, Olly looked at Doctor Feng. She had the curious feeling that he had also recognised the symbol. 'Is there any way of finding out what that means?' she asked him, nodding towards the sheet of paper with the pictogram on it.

'There are over fifty-six thousand characters in Chinese writing,' Doctor Feng said. 'Many of them are no longer used. I suspect this pictogram is some ancient character which has been adopted by a criminal gang. It is clear that they saw what Josh had found and stole it to sell.'

'I'm sure you're right,' said Olly's father. 'There's a lucrative international market in stolen antiquities, more's the pity.'

'Well, let's hope they're caught quickly,' said Olly's gran. 'I shall sleep a lot easier in my bed once I know they're all under lock and key.'

At that moment, the door to the cabin opened and Mr Lau stepped inside. He walked up to the table where they were sitting. 'I have informed Professor Andryanova of the incident with the two young people this afternoon,' he said. 'He has instructed me to tell you that you are all to consider yourselves under my protection from now on.'

Jonathan frowned at him. 'Meaning what?' he asked.

Lau smiled coldly. 'Meaning that no one should leave the site without informing me first,' he said. 'My men will be on guard twenty-four hours a day.' He looked at Olly and Josh. 'And from now on, I suggest that if the two young people want to go out for any reason, they should be accompanied by one of my men.'

Olly glared at him in annoyance. The idea that she and Josh wouldn't be able to set foot outside their cabin without one of Lau's men on their tail did not appeal to her one little bit.

'We will do as you ask, of course, Mr Lau,'

Professor Christie agreed. 'And I'm grateful for your concern over the welfare of Josh and my daughter.' He frowned. 'I intend to begin working tomorrow morning in the areas that my assistant has secured.' He looked at Lau. 'I trust your men won't get in the way?'

Lau nodded briefly. 'Your work will not be impeded, I can assure you,' he said. He gave another curt nod and left.

Olly looked at her father. 'Do we *really* have to ask his permission every time we want to go out?' she asked.

'It's probably best for the time being,' replied the professor. 'Doctor Feng has been in contact with the authorities at Chengdu, and we're hoping some officials will be here tomorrow or the day after. They will be better able to advise us of how we should behave.'

'Meanwhile, perhaps it would be best if Josh and Olly went away?' Mrs Beckmann suggested. 'I could take them to stay in Chengdu while you finish the dig.'

'No!' Olly and Josh chorused in dismay.

Olly looked imploringly at her gran. 'We won't be in any danger with Mr Lau's men on guard,' she said and turned to her father. 'Please don't send us away. It's just not fair. We'll miss everything!'

Professor Christie looked thoughtfully at Olly and Josh. 'No,' he said at length. 'I won't send you to Chengdu – not for the time being anyway.'

Olly and Josh looked at one another in huge relief.

'It's a pity that Josh didn't come and tell us about that golden disc when he first saw it,' Jonathan commented, eyeing his younger brother with a frown.

Josh's forehead wrinkled. 'I'm sorry,' he said. 'I should have done, but I was so excited that I didn't really think.'

'We won't worry about that now,' Professor Christie put in. 'What's done is done.' He looked at Josh. 'Can you remember any of the markings? You said they looked like they showed the plan of a city?'

'I only had a minute or two before I was grabbed,' Josh began, 'but it looked like the city was much bigger than the ruins we've found so far – and the main part of it seemed to be further away from the river. I couldn't quite make it out, but it seemed to have a wall around it.'

'What kind of wall?' Olly asked.

Josh shrugged. 'It was just a couple of lines running right around the main part of the city. I'm not saying it was definitely a wall. I suppose it could have been a big road or a moat or a ditch or something like that. But the water channel was definitely shown – the one under the building.'

'That building is certainly no more than five or six hundred years old,' Jonathan said. 'It can't have been part of the original city. I think it was probably a mill of some kind, built later, over the existing waterway.'

'It wasn't on the plan,' Josh confirmed. 'But what is the water channel? Where does it come from?'

'I should think it's a natural tributary of the river,' the professor replied. 'Probably sourced from a spring in the mountain.'

'But it isn't natural,' Olly pointed out. 'It's made of stone – you just can't see much of that now because of all the mud and stuff.'

'Ah, well, you see, the people who built the city would have constructed an artificial channel to control the flow of the water,' Professor Christie explained. 'We will investigate it further, when we have time,' he continued. 'But our priority must be to get all the information we can from the ruins in the riverbed while we have the chance.'

Olly said goodnight to Josh and went into her room. She opened her travelling bag and withdrew a cherished new piece of electronic equipment that her gran had bought her only a few weeks ago. It was a digital recorder. All she had to do was press a button and speak into the microphone slot each evening, and she would soon have a digitally-recorded diary of the entire dig.

She yawned, worn out by the events of the extraordinary day. She had made her first entry last night, describing their long flight and arrival on site. She had intended to add an update every evening, but now she just wanted to throw her pyjamas on and climb between the sheets. She put the recorder down, deciding that she would record her update in the morning.

She was just about to get undressed when something at the head of the bed caught her eye. A small, black, oblong shape was lying on her pillow. Puzzled, she walked over for a closer look.

To Olly's surprise, the small black oblong was

the mobile phone that the masked man had taken from her in the secret tunnel.

And tied around it was a slender ribbon of red silk.

Chapter Seven

A Secret Revealed

Olly threw Josh's door open and waved the mobile phone at him. 'They brought it back!' she yelled. 'I'm going to tell Dad.' Without waiting for him, she pelted across to the dining cabin. Professor Christie, Jonathan and Audrey Beckmann were still there, talking at the table.

Olly ran in and thumped the phone down in front of her father. 'I found it on my pillow,' she said. 'What kind of thieves give things back?' She stared around at the startled faces. Moments later, Josh arrived, barefoot, wearing jeans and his pyjama top.

The return of Olly's mobile phone caused surprise and puzzlement to everyone. No one could make sense of it.

'We'll have to let Mr Lau know,' Jonathan said. 'Whoever put it in Olly's room must have walked right past his guards.' He snorted. 'So much for his protection!'

But the question still remained: if the masked men were a band of thieves, then why return something that they could have sold? Even if they were thieves intent only on stealing the golden disc, why not just throw the mobile phone away? Why take the risk of coming right into the camp to give it back?

'We're obviously not going to get to the bottom of this tonight,' said Mrs Beckmann. 'Jonathan, could you go and tell Mr Lau what has happened? Suggest to him that his men need to be far more vigilant from now on.' She looked at Olly and Josh. 'You two should go back to bed,' she said. 'I'm sure there won't be any more unwelcome visitors, but I want you to keep the doors and windows shut and locked.' She stood up. 'Off you go now, and get some sleep.'

As the two friends headed back to their cabin, Olly looked thoughtful. 'If you ask me, they brought my phone back to show us that they aren't just a bunch of thieves.'

Josh stared at her in disbelief. 'They kidnapped us and locked us up, remember?' he demanded.

'But they didn't hurt us, did they?' Olly pointed out. 'And they left food and water for us. For all we know, they might have come back and let us out once they'd hidden the golden disc away.' She looked at Josh's dubious face. 'I think that was all they wanted – the golden disc.'

Josh frowned but didn't reply. Olly had given him a lot to think about.

It was a long time before Olly was able to sleep. She lay in her darkened room, staring wide-eyed at the ceiling, trying to make sense of it all. She toyed absently with the red ribbon, while her mind raced. She knew that foreigners often considered Chinese people to be inscrutable – but this was ridiculous!

She eventually drifted off, still no closer to understanding the motives of the extraordinary kidnappers, who had risked capture in order to return her stolen phone.

It was very strange.

* * *

Josh's sleep was also disturbed, but he was puzzling over something else – something which he had not remembered until now.

The plan on the golden disc had seemed to show that the lost city was divided into two sections. There was a small outpost on the banks of the river, and then a much larger area behind, presumably built up in the foothills of the mountain. But the important point was that the two parts of the city were linked by the water channel. Josh lay in the dark and thought that, if the waterway was tracked back towards the mountain, surely it would lead to a lot more of the lost city, lying undiscovered, maybe only a few centimetres below the earth.

He finally fell asleep, imagining himself finding the first piece of masonry that would lead to the spectacular discovery of the whole of Yueliang-Chengshi.

By the time Josh woke up the next morning, Jonathan was already up and out. Josh dressed and went to Olly's room. He found her sitting fully-clothed on her bed and talking into her digital recorder. She pressed the stop button and listened as he told her what he had remembered about the plan on the golden disc.

Her eyes lit up as he spoke. 'We should follow the channel all the way back and see exactly where it goes,' she said excitedly.

Josh nodded. 'That's exactly what I think,' he agreed. 'I'm going to tell Jonathan and the professor about it right now.'

Olly shook her head. 'No, I mean *we* should follow it – you and I,' she said. 'I'm sure Dad will want to investigate the watercourse the first chance he gets, but right now everyone's concentrating on the buildings on the riverbank. So why don't we keep quiet about it and do some exploring on our own?'

'Because last time we went off on our own, we both got kidnapped,' Josh pointed out. 'They'll never let us out alone.'

Olly smiled. 'But we won't be alone,' she said. 'We'll be together.'

Josh's face broke into a broad grin as he looked at her. 'The waterway runs off towards the mountains. In order to follow it, we'll have to get off the site without anyone noticing,' he said. 'And that means getting past Mr Lau's men.'

'We can outwit them,' Olly said confidently. 'No problem.'

Josh nodded. 'Of course we can,' he said. Then he frowned. 'But if we see anything suspicious out there, we run for it, OK?'

'OK,' Olly agreed.

There was the sound of footsteps in the adjoining room. A moment later, Audrey Beckmann put her head round the door. 'Lessons in thirty minutes,' she said. 'You just have time for breakfast. Don't be late.'

Olly looked at her. 'You do remember that today is the Festival of the Moon, don't you?' she said. 'It's a public holiday in China – people take the day off, you know. So, I was wondering . . .'

'Nice try, Olly,' Mrs Beckmann broke in. 'But you're still doing your schoolwork this morning.'

As it turned out, Olly's gran had come up with something special that day. A large part of the morning's lesson was devoted to Chinese history and to information about the Moon Festival.

Olly and Josh learnt that the festival always took place on the fifteenth day of the eighth month of the Chinese lunar calendar – the Chicken Month.

Although it was held to celebrate the moon goddess, Chang-O, it was also a celebration of the harvest.

'We are going to be able to go to the festival, aren't we?' Olly asked.

Mrs Beckmann nodded. 'We'll all go together to Chung-Hsien this evening,' she said. 'The festivities don't really get going until after nightfall. Not that the farmers around here have a great deal to celebrate this year. Still, I expect they'll make the best of it. Apparently, the dragon dance and the lion dance are especially interesting. The dragon dance is supposed to protect the people from sickness and disease, but the lion dance is meant to bring rain.' She looked at them. 'And I'm sure they will be hoping the lion does his job particularly well this year,' she finished.

After lunch, Josh and Olly went to their cabin. Mrs Beckmann had driven into Chung-Hsien for some provisions – and she wasn't expected back for several hours. Practically everyone else was busy in the ruins. Jonathan and a small team were putting the last safety measures in place, but the rest of the site was now being excavated. Occasionally, diggers would make their way to the finds hut, carefully carrying newly-excavated items – but apart from that, the only people near the huts were a couple of Lau's men, standing guard. Josh borrowed his brother's binoculars, then went to join Olly in her room.

'How are we going to get past them?' Josh asked, watching one of Lau's men from the window. 'They probably won't pay any attention to us while we're on site – but as soon as they see us following the watercourse off into the hills, they'll stop us for sure.'

'Then we have to make sure they don't see us,' Olly said. She pointed. 'Do you see that line of boulders off behind the dining cabin?' Josh looked where she was indicating. Several large rocks jutted out from the dry grey mud. 'If we can get down behind them, we can use them as cover all the way up the bank,' Olly went on. 'Then all we have to do is get to the other side of that hill and we'll be out of sight.'

Josh looked dubiously at the long bare hillside. 'If any of Lau's men happen to look in that direction while we're on the slope, they'll definitely spot us,' he said.

'There's no other way,' Olly replied. 'Unless you think we should go and ask their permission.'

Josh shook his head. 'Let's do it,' he said. 'I just hope we find something to make this worthwhile.'

'We will,' Olly said. 'I've just got a feeling we will.'

They slipped out of the cabin and made their way carefully through the camp without being seen. Olly pressed against the wall of one of the storage huts and peered quickly around the corner. 'OK,' she said softly. 'I can see one of Lau's men, but he's facing the other way. I'll make a dash for the rocks, then you follow once I'm safe.'

Before Josh could speak, she had gone. He watched from cover as she ran at a crouch towards the line of boulders. She threw herself on to the ground behind them. The guard had seen nothing.

Taking a deep breath, Josh raced after her, expecting to hear a shout from behind him at any moment. He reached the boulders and ducked down out of sight.

Olly was grinning. 'Piece of mooncake!' she said. 'Now, follow me, and keep your head down.' She crawled up the dry riverbank with Josh close at her heels.

A minute or so later, they had come to the end of the natural cover. They were above the line of the river and ahead of them was a bare slope about twenty metres long. As Olly had said, once they were on the other side, they would be able to use the natural contours of the land to make their way unseen to the watercourse, but as Josh stared up the slope, it seemed a long way to run.

Olly lifted her head cautiously over the rock. 'It's OK,' she whispered. 'He's still looking the other way. Let's go!' She took off like a gazelle, racing madly up the slope. Josh was after her in a moment. He risked a quick glance over his shoulder. The guard was still facing the other way. It looked like they were going to make it.

Olly leapt over the crest of the hill and made a slithering landing on the far side, skidding down in a cloud of dust. Josh dropped down just behind the ridge, panting from his run. He lifted his head over the crest, wanting to be absolutely certain that they had not been seen.

His heart jumped into his mouth. The guard had turned. He was staring towards the hill. Had he seen them? The man had his radio in his hand and was obviously speaking to someone.

Josh ducked down again and slithered to join Olly at the foot of the hill. 'He saw us!' he gasped.

She stared at him. 'Is he coming?'

'I don't know,' Josh replied. 'He was talking on the radio.'

An anxious look clouded Olly's face. 'Perhaps we should go back?' she suggested.

'Not after you've dragged me this far,' Josh told her. 'Come on, let's get out of here before they turn up.'

She blinked at him and then grinned. 'Great idea.'

They ran side by side along the narrow valley between two ridges of land. Keeping always to the low ground, they quickly made their way up from the river and closer to the sacred mountain.

They lay on one of the higher slopes and finally risked lifting their heads to peep over the top. They had come several hundred metres from the river. The folds of the land prevented them from being able to see most of the ruins of the city – but away to their right, they could see what remained of the old mill building. Their plan was to pick up the watercourse behind the mill, and then follow it back into the hills to its source. There was no sign of pursuit.

'I told you we'd lose them,' Olly said with a laugh, scrambling back down the slope.

'We still have to get back without getting caught,' Josh reminded her.

She looked at him, her eyes gleaming. 'We won't have to worry about that if we find something spectacular,' she said.

Still keeping low, they made their way towards the back of the old mill.

At last they were standing on the high bank, looking at the rushing water as it flowed down from the hills and into the mill. Josh pointed to the rear wall of the building. A dark stain ran along the stonework, several metres above the point where the water poured from an arched entrance. 'That must be the normal level of the water,' he remarked. Then he looked up into the distance from where the stream came. The deep waterway stretched off between the rising hills as far as the eye could see.

Josh climbed to higher ground. He put the binoculars to his eyes, trying to make out where the canal came from – but the folds of the land were in the way. 'We'll have to follow it,' he called down to Olly. 'I can't see where it comes from.'

A sharp voice carried to Josh on the breeze. He turned quickly, staring over his shoulder. Lau was standing on a high bank of land, about fifty metres away, with his back to Josh. He was holding a mobile phone or a radio to his ear. He made wide gestures as he spoke, and his words sounded like commands. Josh got the strong impression that he was giving orders to his men – organising a hunt for himself and Olly.

Josh dropped to the ground, his head low, watching intently. Lau gave more orders and beckoned sharply. Moments later, a second man joined him on the hilltop.

Josh slithered helter-skelter down the hillside.

'What's wrong?' Olly asked.

'They're getting close,' Josh gasped.

Olly's eyes widened. 'We better get out of sight,' she said. She pointed to the bank below them. 'We can hide there.' The bank was undercut, leaving an overhang of earth matted with dry grass. They dropped down on to the steep slope of the canal and scrambled under the dry turf.

Josh's heart was hammering in his chest as he lay there on the ground. He held his breath, listening intently. It wasn't long before he heard the voices of two men speaking rapidly together in Mandarin. They were close – too close.

Lau's voice sounded directly overhead. Josh realised Lau must be standing on the lip of earth right above his hiding place. Dirt rained down over Josh's face, but he didn't dare wipe it away in case the movement was heard.

Lau shouted something and received a faint reply from some distance away. It was impossible to tell what the men were saying, but Josh assumed that they were trying to work out where the two friends had disappeared to.

Then the tone of Lau's voice changed – as if he was speaking to someone much closer by – and Josh realised with surprise that Lau was now speaking in English.

'Yes, sir, we think the two of them may well have found something of significance. We're close behind them. They cannot have gone far. We'll find them,' he said.

Josh thought at first that he must be speaking on a mobile phone to Professor Christie or to Jonathan – although Lau had never called either of them 'sir'. But then Lau's words took a strange turn.

'No, sir, we don't have any more news about the disc – we have people searching for it. Yes, it's only a matter of time.' A pause, and then he said something which made Josh catch his breath. 'We will do everything we can to locate the disc, Mr Cain. Leave it to us.'

Josh's brain reeled with shock. He wondered whether he had misheard. Could Lau really be talking to Ethan Cain?

Chapter Eight

Pursuit

Olly lay perfectly still in the confines of her narrow hiding place – but her brain was whirling. She had heard Lau speaking on the mobile phone, and leapt to the same conclusion as Josh – the security chief was talking to Ethan Cain!

She listened as the second man joined Lau and they spoke in Mandarin for a few moments. Then they moved off. As far as Olly could tell they headed down the waterway towards the old mill.

'Olly!' It was a frantic whisper from Josh. 'Did you hear what I heard?'

Olly squirmed out of her hiding place and climbed up on to level ground. Josh emerged – covered in dust – and joined her, his eyes wide.

'Ethan Cain!' Olly confirmed grimly.

Josh's eyes narrowed. 'So much for that reclusive Texan oil millionaire,' he said. 'There's probably no such person as Augustus Bell – I bet it's been Ethan Cain all along. I expect he hired Professor Andryanova to run the excavation for him.' Then he frowned. 'But my mother said he wasn't even interested in this dig,' he said. 'She told me he was working flat out on some big project in California. She wouldn't lie to me.'

'No, she wouldn't,' Olly agreed. 'But Ethan wouldn't worry about lying to her! And he knows about the golden disc. Lau must have been passing him information about everything that's been happening.'

Josh let out a low whistle. 'He must think the disc is pretty important for some reason.'

'Maybe he knows something we don't,' Olly suggested.

Josh shook his head. 'How can he? I only found it yesterday.'

'Was Mr Lau around when you were describing it to everyone?' Olly asked.

Josh thought hard. 'Yes,' he replied. 'I think he was.'

'Lau probably got on the phone to Ethan and told him all about it,' Olly said. 'And if Ethan thinks that the plan on the disc might show where the Mooncake of Chang-O is hidden, then he'll want to get his hands on that disc at all costs.'

Josh frowned. 'But why are they following us? We don't have it.'

'No, but maybe he guessed that we'd learnt something from it. Maybe that's why it was so easy for us to get out of the camp – they let us out on purpose. And they weren't following us to drag us back – they wanted to find out where we were going!'

Josh grabbed Olly's arm. 'We have to get back and tell Jonathan and your dad.'

Olly shook her head. 'They won't believe us,' she said.

'Why would we lie about it?' Josh asked.

Olly smiled. 'They won't think we're lying, Josh,' she said. 'They'll just think we've got it all wrong again – like in the Valley of the Kings. Remember how Jonathan reacted a couple of days ago on the aeroplane when I mentioned Ethan Cain? He said we should forget all about the "misunderstanding"! I'm sure Ethan has given Mr Lau orders to keep his involvement totally secret. If we go charging in there telling them all that Augustus Bell is really Ethan Cain, they'll just think we've gone potty.'

Josh looked thoughtfully at her. 'And we can't prove it, can we?'

She shook her head. 'No, we can't.'

Josh kicked frustratedly at a stone. It tumbled down the steeply curved bank and splashed into the water. 'Well, what *can* we do, then?' he asked.

'We can find out where this water comes from,' Olly said firmly. 'That's what we came out here to do – so let's do it.' She looked at him. 'And let's hope we find something to lead us to the Mooncake of Chang-O before Ethan's men get there. Because that's what he's after, Josh – he wants the talisman, and it's up to us to make sure he doesn't get it.'

They followed the slow winding of the watercourse up through the rising hills. As the ground became rougher, the canal pushed its way between high shoulders of bare rock. Sometimes they had to climb away from the canal to find a route through. Here and there, they saw places where there had been land-slips into the canal – leaving rocks and boulders and earth banks around which the rapid water swirled and foamed.

'How far do you think we've come?' Olly asked, eventually.

'I don't know,' Josh replied. He looked at his watch. It was mid-afternoon. They had been out of the camp for nearly two hours. 'Do you think we should be getting back?'

'Not just yet.' Olly found a high point and lay on the top, scanning the land ahead of them with the binoculars. Josh kept watch on the way they had come. So far they had been lucky and remained undetected, but he was convinced that Lau and his men were still out there somewhere, scouring the hills for them.

Olly tracked the course of the canal and caught sight of something odd in the distance. She couldn't quite make it out. Then she realised what she was looking at. At first glance, it seemed as if the waterway ran straight out of a cliff-face, but as she focused more carefully, she saw that the water was pouring out of a black archway made of set stones. And she could even see that there was a kind of raised ridge alongside the rushing water – like a pathway – that led under the arch and into the mountain.

'Josh,' she called down, her voice breathless with

suppressed excitement. 'The canal goes into a tunnel.'

'What kind of tunnel?' Josh asked, climbing up to where she lay.

'See for yourself.' She handed him the binoculars. He put them to his eyes.

'That can't be natural, can it?' Olly said. 'Someone must have made it.'

Josh nodded. 'Let's find out where it goes,' he suggested eagerly.

A shout broke the still air. Startled, they both turned. One of Lau's men was standing on a ridge of rock above them. He gestured to them – a signal that plainly meant they should stay where they were. Then he began to clamber down the hillside towards them. A few moments later, a second man appeared against the skyline and followed suit.

Olly looked at Josh. 'Do you want to stay here and get marched back to camp by Ethan Cain's goons?' she challenged. 'Or do you want to lose them and find out where that tunnel goes?'

Josh took a final glance at the two approaching men, then grinned at Olly. 'Let's lose them,' he replied.

The two friends ran along the canalside, searching for a place where they could cross without having to swim. There were more shouts from behind them. They came to a place where a whole chunk of the hillside had crumbled away, strewing rocks and boulders into the canal. Olly went first, jumping from boulder to boulder, arms spread for balance. She glanced over her shoulder and saw that Josh was right behind her.

The two men shouted again. Olly ignored them. 'We have to lead them away from the tunnel,' she called to Josh breathlessly. 'They mustn't find out about it. They'll tell Ethan.'

She jumped on to a rock that was just under the surface of the rushing water. But the stone was slippery. Her foot slid from under her and she fell into the water. Josh dropped to his knees and snatched at her, catching hold of her arm. But he didn't have time to get a sure footing, and her weight sent him, too, slithering off the rock and into the fast-flowing water.

Shaking water from their eyes, they swam to the far bank and scrambled out.

'Are you OK?' Josh asked.

'No, I'm not!' Olly snapped, obviously annoyed

with herself. 'Look at me – I'm soaked! Now what do we do?'

'I've had an idea,' Josh replied. 'Come with me – I know where we can go.' He scrambled up the hillside and down the far slope. Olly followed.

'Where are we going?' Olly gasped as they ran.

'Banping!' Josh told her. 'The village where Ang-Lun told us his grandmother lives. It's in this direction – it can't be far away.'

'Ang-Lun will help us lose those creeps,' Olly said, her voice brightening. 'Good thinking, Josh.'

Josh looked back as he reached a hilltop. The two men were still following. They must have made the jump from rock to rock across the canal. And from a different direction, he now saw Lau running towards them too.

'There it is!' called Olly. Josh turned back. Below them, nestling in the foothills under the shadow of the mountain, was a small village of huddled, grey-walled buildings with roofs of split bamboo.

Olly and Josh hurtled down the hillside and ran into the village. An elderly woman, dressed in loose blue overalls and carrying a battered kettle smiled and stared at them with interest, her dark eyes bright under a blue turban. A man in faded denims also stopped to stare, and a woman in a long red dress, carrying a baby, paused at the door of a house and called something back to those inside.

'Ang-Lun!' Olly shouted. *'Qing! Qing!'* Please! Please!

An old man stepped towards them, speaking rapidly and pointing towards a house at one side.

'Ang-Lun?' Josh asked.

'Ang-Lun,' the man responded, nodding. *'Song-Ai-Mi!'*

'I'm sorry, I don't understand,' Josh said.

The man pointed to the house, repeating the same words. *'Song-Ai-Mi.'*

And then, to Josh and Olly's relief and delight, Ang-Lun himself appeared at the door of the house. He ran out to meet them, his face surprised and puzzled. 'You're wet,' Ang-Lun said. 'What happened to you?'

'We'll explain later,' Olly promised. 'Can you hide us?'

'What's wrong?' Ang-Lun asked.

'Lau and some of his men are following us,' Josh explained. 'We don't want them to find us.'

Ang-Lun nodded. 'Come with me.' He ran back into the house with Josh and Olly at his heels. They came into a small room with a brick floor and simple bamboo furniture. The white walls were decorated with hanging scrolls – some covered with Chinese script, others with beautiful, intricate illustrations.

'Stay here, out of sight,' Ang-Lun said, and then he stepped out into the open again and walked on to the dusty street. He turned and looked in the direction from which Olly and Josh had come. Lau and his two men were in sight now, running at a trot down the hillside towards the village.

Olly and Josh watched from the window as Lau and his men approached their Chinese friend. Lau spoke in English, his voice harsh. 'Where are they?'

Ang-Lun shook his head and replied in his own language.

'Speak English,' said Lau. 'I don't understand your dialect.'

'You are not welcome here,' Ang-Lun said in English. 'Go away.' He made a dismissive gesture, as if ordering the men to leave the village.

Lau gave a hard bark of laughter. The men walked towards Ang-Lun. Olly held her breath, wondering what would happen next – wondering to what lengths Lau would be prepared to go in his hunt for her and Josh.

Ang-Lun stood his ground as the three men approached him.

'I have to take the girl and the boy back to camp,' Lau said. 'It's for their own safety. Tell me where they are, or I'll search this entire village.'

Ang-Lun stared defiantly into Lau's face. He spat out a single word. It wasn't English.

Lau's eyes blazed. Olly got the impression he understood that word, just fine – and didn't like it at all! He snatched at Ang-Lun's clothes, grabbing him by the collar. 'We aren't leaving this place until we've found them. Now tell me where they are, or do you want me to beat the truth out of you?'

Ang-Lun glared up fearlessly at Lau's angry face.

'We can't let them hurt him,' Olly cried. 'We've got to stop this.' She and Josh moved to the doorway and stepped outside.

'We're here,' Olly called. 'Let him go!'

Chapter Nine

The Shan-Ren

Lau and his men turned at the sound of Olly's voice. A look of cold satisfaction crossed Lau's face. He gave a curt nod. 'You'll come with us,' he said.

There was nothing else to be done, Olly thought. They had been caught, and now they would be taken back to camp to face the music. She realised that she and Josh had nothing to show for their illicit expedition into the hills. They didn't even dare tell anyone what they *had* found, because once Lau knew about the mysterious tunnel into the mountainside, he would waste no time in telling Ethan Cain. However Olly looked at it, things were not going to go well for them when they got back to camp.

The two friends were about to walk over and join Lau, when Ang-Lun tore free of Lau's grip and stepped back with a loud cry.

Suddenly the small street was full of movement. Men and women appeared in doorways and from between buildings. Some of them were carrying sticks and farm tools. All of them were staring at Lau and his companions.

Olly and Josh looked round in surprise.

'I told you that you are not welcome here,' Ang-Lun said simply. 'Olly and Josh are our guests. They do not want to go with you. Turn around and leave while you can.'

Lau grimaced and made a lunge at Ang-Lun, who jumped back out of reach. There was a rising murmur from the crowd of villagers. One man threw a pitchfork. It stuck in the dry ground only a couple of metres from Lau, the bamboo shaft quivering.

Lau looked around, clearly assessing the situation. The villagers were slowly closing in on the three security men, and many of them held potential weapons in their hands. Lau must have decided he didn't want a pitched battle, for he turned towards Olly and Josh, his mouth set in a tight, grim line of resignation.

'We're fine here for the time being, Mr Lau,' Olly said to him cheerfully. 'You needn't worry about us.'

Lau didn't reply. The circle of villagers had now almost completely surrounded him and his men, leaving them only one clear exit from the village – back the way they had come. Lau turned and walked away without another word. His men followed. As Lau walked back up into the hills, Olly saw that he was already speaking on his mobile phone.

'I wonder who he's talking to,' she murmured to Josh. 'Someone back at camp? Or Ethan Cain?'

Ang-Lun said something to the villagers and they laughed, looking kindly at Olly and Josh. They had obviously enjoyed the brief confrontation.

'What did you call Lau that made him so mad?' Josh asked Ang-Lun.

'*Zei*,' Ang-Lun said with a grin. 'It means bandit.'

'Thanks for getting rid of him for us,' Olly said.

'Come inside again and meet my grandmother,' Ang-Lun suggested. 'And then you can explain why you didn't want to go with Lau – and why you're both so wet.'

Ang-Lun led them through into a second room. A small, elderly woman knelt at a low desk. She looked at Josh and Olly with the same amiable curiosity they had seen in the faces of the other villagers. Her skin was tanned and wrinkled and her dark eyes were bright. She was dressed in an orange tunic and trousers, and her grey hair was cropped close to her head. In front of her was a sheet of red paper and a pot of black ink. She was using a brush to paint beautiful Chinese pictograms on to the paper. As in the first room, Olly saw that the walls through here were hung with writings and illustrations.

The old lady stood up, smiling and nodding at Olly and Josh as Ang-Lun spoke to her. She said something to them, holding out a small, fragile hand for them to shake.

'My grandmother asks if you would like to take tea,' Ang-Lun explained. 'She says we should sit on the terrace where the sun will dry your clothes.'

'That would be lovely,' Olly replied. 'And can you please thank her for the gift she made us? Tell her it's on my bedroom wall.'

Ang-Lun's grandmother smiled and nodded again, as Ang-Lun led Olly and Josh into a little sunny courtyard behind the house. There was a small, low table and some stools.

While they waited for the tea, Olly and Josh told Ang-Lun about their adventure and the archway in the mountainside from which the canal water flowed.

'I didn't even know it existed,' Ang-Lun told them, obviously fascinated. 'It must be very old.'

'That's what we think,' Josh said. 'When the waterway is at its normal level, the arch would be completely submerged. It probably hasn't been seen for hundreds of years.'

'That's why we didn't want Lau and his henchmen to know about it,' Olly added. 'He'll tell Ethan Cain and then there'll be a whole world of trouble.'

Ang-Lun looked puzzled.

'We'd better explain about Ethan,' Josh put in. He told Ang-Lun of their previous encounter with the Californian billionaire, and of his attempt to get the Tears of Isis. 'He's trying to do the same thing here, we're sure of it,' he finished.

'But the real problem is that no one believes us,' Olly continued. 'They all think Ethan is a decent guy.' She looked at Josh. 'We can't tell anyone back at camp about the tunnel,' she said. 'If we tell them, then Lau will find out, too. And once Lau knows, he'll be straight on the phone to Ethan! We can't risk it.'

'So what's the plan?' Josh asked.

'We have to investigate the tunnel ourselves,' Olly said. 'If there's anything important to be found in there, then we need to find it first.'

Josh looked at his watch. 'Your gran will be back from Chung-Hsien soon, if she's not already,' he remarked. 'She's bound to notice we're missing, and they'll all go crazy if they think we've both disappeared again.'

'Yes, we should go back to camp soon,' Olly agreed. 'But we'll slip away and investigate that tunnel the first chance we get.'

Ang-Lun's grandmother came out of the house with a bamboo tray in her hands. On it stood a delicate china teapot and four small white china bowls, patterned with brightly-coloured curling dragons. A few moments later, Olly and Josh were sipping the fragrant green tea.

'Did your father tell you about the golden disc?' Josh asked Ang-Lun.

Ang-Lun nodded. 'He believes it was stolen by bandits.'

'If we draw the symbol the thieves had on their

scarves, do you think your grandmother might know what it means?' Josh enquired.

'She might,' Ang-Lun replied. 'I'll go and get something for you to draw with.'

After a moment, he returned with brush, ink and paper. Josh took the brush and dipped it in the ink. Carefully, he drew the curious lying-down E and upside-down Y symbol.

The old lady looked at it and then gave Olly and Josh a strange, inquisitive glance. '*Shan-Ren,*' she said. Then she turned to Ang-Lun and said some more in her own language.

Ang-Lun's eyes widened as he listened. 'My grandmother says this is the symbol of the Shan-Ren – the guardians of the mountain,' he told Josh and Olly.

Josh looked at him, puzzled. 'I thought you told us they died out centuries ago.'

Ang-Lun spoke again to his grandmother. Her reply seemed to surprise him.

'What is she saying?' Olly asked eagerly.

Ang-Lun smiled at her. 'She said – I'm not quite sure how to translate it – she said that old trees have deep roots.'

Olly blinked at him. 'Excuse me?'

'I know what she means!' Josh exclaimed. 'The Shan-Ren didn't die out – they just went underground.' He looked at Ang-Lun. 'You said that the Shan-Ren were the guardians of the mountain. But why does the mountain need to be guarded?'

Ang-Lun translated Josh's question for his grandmother.

She shook her head. '*Laocheng*,' she said. '*Mimi! Mimi!*' She smiled at Olly and laughed softly.

'My grandmother says it is a secret – I'm afraid she won't tell you,' Ang-Lun explained.

Josh looked thoughtfully at the old lady. 'If the disc was taken by the Shan-Ren, then perhaps they thought there was something on it that gave the secret away,' he mused.

'What secret?' Olly asked. And then she reached out and gripped Josh's arm as an astonishing thought struck her. 'What if the secret is the location of the Mooncake of Chang-O?' she said. 'What if that disc wasn't just a street plan – what if it was a *treasure map*?' She fixed Josh with a fierce gaze. 'You have to remember everything you can about that plan – every little detail.'

Josh bit his lip as he struggled to remember. 'It

showed part of the town near the river. And then the rest of the city a little way away, surrounded by some kind of thick wall or something. That's about it.'

A car horn suddenly blared from the street outside, interrupting the conversation.

'What's that?' Olly asked Ang-Lun.

'I'll go and see,' Ang-Lun replied. 'You wait here.' He disappeared into the house.

His grandmother was watching Olly with her bright dark eyes.

'*Xiexie*,' Olly said carefully, pointing to the tea. Thank you.

The old lady smiled and gave a slight bow of her head. Then they heard footsteps in the house, coming towards the back door, and they all looked round.

Olly's gran stood in the doorway, her face grim. Olly opened her mouth to speak, but Mrs Beckmann raised her hand. 'Thank Ang-Lun's grandmother for her hospitality,' she said, her voice very calm and controlled. 'Then come with me to the car.' She turned and walked back through the house.

Olly and Josh looked at each other, and Olly

swallowed. She had never seen her gran looking quite so angry before. 'We are in big trouble!' she said.

Chapter Ten

Into the Tunnel

All the way back to camp, Olly and Josh waited for the axe to fall, but Olly's gran was worryingly silent. It was not until they arrived that they learnt what their punishment was to be.

'Not only did you leave the camp when you were expressly told to stay put,' Mrs Beckmann said in a cold fury, 'but you enlisted the help of Ang-Lun to make a fool of Mr Lau. You have probably stirred up who knows what resentments between the villagers and Mr Lau's men – and you've made a difficult situation a great deal worse.' Her eyes blazed. 'You will not be coming to the festival with us this evening. I'm sorry I have to be so hard with you both, but you must learn to obey the rules.'

Neither of them argued.

Jonathan was sympathetic when he heard. 'You are a pair of idiots sometimes,' he said later, when they were alone with him in their cabin. 'What made you wander off like that when you know there are dangerous people out there?'

'But they aren't dangerous,' Olly argued. 'The men who took the golden disc are Shan-Ren. They weren't going to hurt us. They just wanted to keep their secret.'

Jonathan frowned. 'The Shan-Ren died out centuries ago,' he said. 'Where did you get all this nonsense?'

'Ang-Lun's gran recognised the pictogram on their scarves,' Josh explained. 'She seemed very sure that it was the symbol of the Shan-Ren.'

'And because some people decide to wear the same symbol, you assume they're members of an ancient secret society that doesn't even exist any more, is that it?' Jonathan questioned incredulously. He shook his head. 'And anyway, what were you doing out near the mountain?'

Olly and Josh exchanged a quick glance. 'We were, er, exploring,' Olly said lamely.

'We wanted to find out where the canal went,' Josh added.

'And did you?' Jonathan asked.

'Not really,' Olly replied quickly, before Josh could respond to his brother's question. 'We didn't have time. Lau and his men found us.'

'And that's another thing I don't understand,' Jonathan declared. 'Why run away from Lau? What did you think it would achieve?'

'We don't like being followed around,' Josh said. 'And we don't like Lau.'

'He's not here to be likeable,' Jonathan retorted. 'He's here to protect us.' He shook his head. 'You're acting like little kids.'

Olly felt a rush of blood to her face. She hated that Jonathan should think badly of them. 'Lau isn't what he pretends to be,' she murmured.

'What on earth does that mean?' Jonathan demanded.

Olly looked at him. She desperately wanted to tell him the whole story – how Lau was working for Ethan Cain, and how she and Josh were absolutely convinced that Ethan was manipulating people to find the Mooncake of Chang-O for him. But she couldn't. She knew Jonathan would not believe her, there would be a terrible row and Jonathan would end up thinking even more badly of herself and

Josh. It was a horrible, hopeless situation.

Then the time came for everyone to leave for Chung-Hsien. Olly watched gloomily from the cabin window as the archaeologists and workers piled into four-by-fours. 'I hope they have a nice time,' she muttered dully.

Josh sat on the edge of her bed, resting his chin on his hand. He couldn't even bear to watch.

The only ones left at camp were Lau's men – and Olly and Josh. Olly sighed as the vehicles drove out of sight. She could see one of the security men on the riverbank nearby, and another standing over by the ruins. She knew that there were others dotted about the site, including one standing right outside the cabin door.

Olly stalked the room like a caged tiger, frustrated that they had been so close to making a major discovery when Lau had caught up with them. She had seen the tunnel from which the water flowed, and there had been a footpath running alongside the rushing water – a footpath that might lead to who knows what wonderful secrets. And now, instead of exploring the tunnel, they were stuck in the cabin with one of Lau's men guarding the entrance. It was maddening.

Josh watched her as she marched to and fro past the bed. 'I've been thinking,' he began. 'It's only going to be a matter of time before someone else spots that tunnel. And as soon as it's found, Lau is bound to tell Ethan all about it.'

Olly nodded gloomily. 'And Ethan will be as keen as we are to know where it goes,' she said. 'So then there'll be a race to see who gets there first – Ethan Cain's people or us.'

'Exactly!' Josh agreed. 'And we have to make sure it's us. So we need to go back there right now! This is the perfect time – while everyone is away. There are still a few hours before the sun goes down – that's plenty of time to get there and take a look around. And the festival doesn't finish till late, so we'll be back here before anyone even realises we're gone.'

'That's a great plan, Josh,' Olly cried. But then her face fell and she pointed to the door. 'But how are we going to get past him?'

Josh frowned. 'That's a good question,' he said. 'Have you got any ideas?'

Olly sat down, looking thoughtful. Then she leapt to her feet again in delight. 'I've got it,' she declared. 'We can play my diary recordings to make the guard think we're still here, meanwhile we slip out of the window and off into the hills!'

'Excellent,' Josh said, getting up. 'Now, help me make the bed so it looks like someone's asleep in it – then we can do the same in my room.' He grinned. 'That way, if the guard gets nosy and decides to check up on us after your recordings have run out, he'll just think we've gone to bed.'

'Josh, if I wasn't worried about you getting a swollen head, I'd say that was almost brilliant,' Olly declared, getting to work on the bedclothes.

A few minutes later all the preparations were in place. Clothes and bags had been bundled up under the bedcovers in both rooms, to give the impression that the beds were occupied, and Josh had found a torch. The only problem was that both their watches were suffering from water-damage, so they'd have to guess the time.

Olly set the digital diary on a chair close to the door and pressed the playback button. Her voice sounded. 'Testing, testing. OK, this is Olly Christie's private and personal diary – so if you're listening to this, you shouldn't be. It's August the fifth and I've just finished packing my stuff for our trip to China. The whole gang is going again, and

I'm really looking forward to it. I'd never tell Josh this, but I really like it when he comes along with us, because . . .'

'OK,' Olly said, bundling Josh towards the window. 'We'd better get going.'

'Wait a minute, I want to hear this,' Josh protested.

'It's private and personal,' Olly said firmly. 'Now get out of that window before I have to push you out.'

Josh climbed through the window and dropped to the ground. A few moments later, Olly let herself down beside him. She reached up and pulled the window closed. She left the catch undone – so they would be able to get back in – but to anyone who didn't look too closely, the window would appear to be shut.

'Right,' Olly whispered. 'Let's go!'

The early-evening sun threw the great mountain into dark shadow as Olly and Josh made their way along the course of the waterway. The old volcano loomed above them, dominating the pale sky; its head, as ever, shrouded in white mist.

They were soon tired from scrambling over the

rocks, but the fear of being seen and followed had lessened as they moved further away from the camp. At last they found the same piece of high ground from which Olly had first seen the tunnel. She put the binoculars to her eyes.

The dark tunnel mouth leapt into her circle of vision. In the late afternoon light under the mountain, the stream of water seemed as black as oil. White crests of foam showed where the flood broke against rocks and earth-banks.

Olly smiled. 'We're almost there,' she said.

They had to slither down a steep incline to reach the place where the water flowed out from the mountain. Here, the land formed a natural bay. From the staining on the rocks, it was clear that the water-level was normally three or four metres higher, and that the tunnel entrance would certainly have been hidden from view.

The stonework had suffered from centuries under running water. Sharp edges had been worn into smooth curves, and here and there a stone had fallen, leaving a black gap. A coldness crept out of the tunnel, making the friends shiver as they stared into the echoing darkness.

Josh switched his torch on. The seething black

water glittered eerily in the light. Olly noticed that the walls of the tunnel had a greenish tinge and roots and stems hung from the curved roof where plants had once forced their way between the stones. A stone-flagged path followed the canal on both sides, stretching away into darkness, beyond the beam of the torch.

'Look!' Olly said, pointing to the key stone in the high arch, two metres above their heads. Carved deep into the time-worn stone, but still clearly visible, was the symbol of the Shan-Ren.

Josh and Olly looked at each other. Then Josh took a deep breath and plunged into the tunnel. With a final glance back at the rosy evening sky, Olly followed.

They soon lost all track of time and distance in the endless night of the tunnel. The half-moon of light from the entrance had gradually dwindled behind them, and now it was gone. All around them as they walked steadily forwards in the light of Josh's torch, the roar of the water echoed and re-echoed.

'How long have we been in here?' Olly asked.

'I don't know,' Josh replied. 'Half an hour?'

'More like an hour, I'd say,' Olly responded. 'How far do you think this tunnel goes?'

Josh turned to look at her. 'Do you want to go back?'

'No. Not yet,' Olly said.

They walked on in silence.

'What's that?' Olly asked after a few moments. The torchlight had picked out a dark slot in the side of the tunnel. It was the first time that they had seen any break in the endless monotony of the stonework.

Josh shone the torch into the gap. 'It's stairs,' he said, aiming the light up a flight of steep, narrow stone steps that rose between walls of solid rock. The treads were uneven and broken in places.

They gazed up the stairway. 'What do we do?' Josh asked. 'Should we keep to the waterway, or see where these stairs go?'

Olly felt torn with indecision. Obviously the stairs had been carved through the solid rock for some purpose, but she was reluctant to abandon the original plan of finding out where the water came from. 'Let's follow the stream for, say, one thousand more steps,' she suggested. 'If we don't find anything by then, we can come back and try the stairs.'

In the event, the decision was forced on them sooner than they had expected. Olly was counting the steps in her head, and she had got to four hundred when Josh stopped in his tracks. She peered ahead and saw that the torchlight had revealed a serious cave-in. The water foamed and bubbled over large chunks of stone and forced its way between them, hissing and splashing. The stone walkways on either side of the stream were completely blocked.

Josh looked at Olly. 'The stairs?' he asked.

She nodded. 'The stairs.'

They returned to the staircase and started up the steps. It was a tricky climb. Olly found it easier to use hands as well as feet on the ancient stones, and more than once she stepped on an edge that crumbled away beneath her foot, almost making her fall. She could hear the loosened stones tumbling down into the well of darkness behind her.

Olly gave up counting steps at three hundred – but then, just as she was wondering if the stairway would ever end, she came to the final step and found herself staring down a long tunnel filled with a strange, silver light.

She sat on the top step, rubbing her aching legs and getting her breath back. Josh joined her, and they gazed along the tunnel together. The curious light was coming from the far end. It didn't seem like daylight – and besides, it must surely be dark outside by now – but Olly couldn't think what else it might be.

Without speaking, they both got up and walked along the passage. After a little while, Josh turned his torch off. The light was strong but hazy. It reminded Olly of car headlights shining through thick fog. And the closer they came to the end of the tunnel, the brighter the light became, until it was almost dazzling.

'Careful!' Josh said suddenly, catching hold of Olly's arm as they came to the tunnel mouth.

Olly looked down at her feet and saw that the stones had come to an abrupt stop. The tunnel appeared to end in a vast misty cliff-face. She couldn't see how far the drop was because wisps of cloud swirled about her feet, obscuring whatever lay below. She glanced up and gave a gasp of wonder. Beyond more shreds of mist, the sky was black above her and filled with bright stars. And overhead, larger than she could ever remember seeing it before, shone the full harvest moon.

But then Olly noticed a dark outer edge to the sky. It curved all around her, sending up black fangs into the net of starlight. 'Josh,' she breathed, her voice trembling. 'We're inside the mountain!'

Josh didn't reply – he was gazing around in awe – but his fingers tightened on her arm.

Now Olly understood the strange silver light. It was the moonlight, shining down upon the layer of cloud that filled the crater of the extinct volcano. They had seen it before – when they had flown over it in broad daylight – but under the full moon, it glowed with a pearly sheen that was like something from another world.

And even as Olly gazed down into the cloud, it drifted as if disturbed by a silent wind. The silvery veil swirled and parted, and for a moment, Olly found herself staring down on to a sight that took her breath away.

Chapter Eleven

Yueliang-Chengshi

Far below, glimpsed fleetingly as the mist lifted, Olly saw buildings. Not broken ruins – but perfect buildings with pearly walls and spiked silver towers and elegant, curved grey roofs.

Then the clouds moved again and the vision was lost.

'Yueliang-Chengshi,' Josh murmured.

Olly stared at him. 'The lost city?'

He nodded. 'It was inside the volcano all the time,' he said. 'Remember the lines I saw around the city plan on the golden disc? I thought it was a wall – but it was actually the mountain!'

Olly stared down into the swirling silver mist. 'This is the secret that the Shan-Ren have been protecting,' she said softly. 'That's why they took the golden disc – they knew it gave away the exact location of this city.' She looked at Josh. 'The Mooncake of Chang-O must be down there somewhere.'

'Yes,' Josh agreed. 'And that's why we have to explore as much of the city as we can before we go back. There's no way this place can be kept secret now, and as soon as we tell Jonathan and your dad about it, Lau will pass the news on to Ethan Cain.'

'You're right,' Olly said. 'And I'm *not* going to let him find the Mooncake first!' She looked around for some way down from the ledge. A narrow, winding stairway of stone, carved into the sheer mountainside, descended into the cloud to one side.

Olly moved to the stairway and took a first cautious step down. The stone held firm under her foot. She began to descend, one hand pressed against the rock-face for support.

Josh was right behind her. 'Watch where you're going,' he said anxiously. 'I don't want to have to explain to your gran if you fall and get splatted.'

Olly pulled a face and concentrated on her descent. She could make out the mountain wall at her side, and a few steps above and below her – but the rest of the world was already disappearing in a dense blanket of bright white cloud. The air was cool and damp against her skin as thick tendrils of vapour curled around her body.

The constant shifting of the mist was disorientating – and it was very disturbing to have to lower herself, step by step, into nothingness – but as she descended, Olly gradually noticed that she could see further. She was coming out under the cloud layer.

And then, quite suddenly it seemed, the mists cleared, and she saw stretching away below her, the fabulous lost city of Yueliang-Chengshi.

Somehow the light of the full moon penetrated the clouds, giving the whole city a lustrous, radiant glow – as though all the buildings were made from trapped and moulded moonlight. There were towers and spires of silver stone, gleaming in the beautiful, luminous light. There were walls that glowed as though with an inner fire. There were minarets and cupolas and soaring pagodas amid streets of silver. And shining courtyards stretched away, filled with statues of men and women and dragons and lions.

But now that Olly was closer to the city, she could see that it was deserted and abandoned. From the high ledge, it had looked perfect under the light of the moon, but from here she could see that much of it was in ruins.

'The cloud is getting thinner,' Josh said. 'That must be why it's so bright down here.'

Olly looked up. Veiled in wisps of cloud, she could see the white disc of the huge full moon. Then she paused as a faint scent reached her. 'Can you smell flowers?' she asked.

Josh sniffed. 'No, I can't smell anything,' he replied.

Olly frowned and sniffed. 'Neither can I now,' she remarked. 'I must have imagined it.'

She walked down the last couple of dozen steps and passed through an ornate archway that led to a wide courtyard of grey stone. It was ringed with statues – life-sized terracotta soldiers wearing full traditional Chinese armour of linked stone discs. Some of the figures were cracked or broken – and many had lost a limb – but of those that were still intact, Olly noticed that every face was different, as if the ancient craftsmen had given each of the men a unique personality.

At the end of the courtyard, a covered gateway was formed by the lean body of a rearing dragon. The creature was carved from white stone, with ivory claws and teeth, and jewelled eyes that glittered like fire. Olly stopped in her tracks, gazing at the beautiful sculpture. But then she caught another whiff of flowers – jasmine, she thought, or possibly lotus blossom. But she could see no flowers of any kind, and then the scent was gone again.

'Did you smell it that time?' she asked Josh.

'No. What?' Josh replied, looking puzzled.

Olly shook her head. 'Nothing,' she murmured. 'It doesn't matter.' She walked on across the courtyard, between the ranks of silent soldiers, with Josh at her side.

'No wonder no one knows this place is here,' he commented, looking up at the thin white veil of cloud. 'We flew right over the mountain and we didn't see a thing.'

Olly looked around. 'It's a very strange place,' she said thoughtfully. 'From above, it looked absolutely perfect – as if people could come walking out of the buildings at any moment. But it's all falling to pieces once you get closer.'

'It's still amazingly well-preserved, though,' Josh said. 'Especially when you think how old it must be.'

Olly's eyes lit up. 'And we're probably the first people to see it for thousands of years,' she said.

Through the dragon gate, they found a building with a forecourt of ornate sculptures. Long-necked birds seemed to be dancing to the music of stone musicians playing exotic instruments.

'Those birds are cranes,' Josh told Olly. 'I've read about them. The ancient Chinese people thought cranes were immortal.'

'Why are musicians playing to them?' Olly asked.

'To keep them happy,' Josh replied. 'So they won't fly away. They believed that if the cranes stayed, then the people would live for ever as well.'

Olly looked at the dancing birds. 'They seem happy enough,' she remarked. She gazed around at the deserted city. 'But it doesn't seem to have worked for the people, does it?'

Pearly water trickled from fountains and ran in narrow rivulets, filling the still air with a soft rippling sound. Olly was just about to move on, when once again she smelled the heady fragrance of flowers. 'This is getting ridiculous,' she muttered, looking around for flowers – still there were none to be seen. 'Where is that smell coming from?'

'Flowers again?' Josh asked. He sniffed deeply.

'Can you smell it now?' Olly enquired hopefully.

Josh frowned. 'I'm not sure. There might be something – but it's very faint.' He shook his head. 'No. It's gone.'

'I've had enough of this,' Olly said. She marched off determinedly. 'I'm going to find those flowers.'

They turned a corner and found themselves on a broad avenue of fabulous palaces. Olly followed the fleeting scent along the silvery roadway that stretched ahead of her. The avenue rose gradually in a long, gentle slope, and at the far end of the street, standing high on a hill of white marble steps, was a solitary building that seemed to be made of shining moonlight.

'I've seen pictures of buildings that look like that,' Josh said. 'I think it's a temple.'

'Let's go and find out,' Olly suggested, her natural curiosity taking over.

Together they walked quickly up the long road and climbed the gleaming marble stairs. The white stone walls of the temple reflected the moonlight, giving the building its dazzling radiance. Carved on the walls, the friends could see moon-symbols inlaid with jade and ebony, turquoise and agate.

'There are some flowers here,' Josh said. He pointed to the pillars and doorposts of the temple, up which stone flowers climbed, inlaid with gems that sparkled in the light.

Olly frowned and leant close to one of the carved blossoms. She sniffed experimentally, but there was no scent. 'Stone flowers don't smell,' she said to herself. 'That's just silly.' But as she passed through the high doorway, she caught the faintest hint of jasmine.

Inside, the ceiling was of black lacquer, inlaid with opalescent stars and a mother-of-pearl moon. The walls were also a lustrous, shining black.

'How has all this survived for so long?' Olly wondered.

'I suppose the volcano has kept the city hidden from humans and protected it from the worst of the weather,' Josh replied.

Olly nodded and moved on through to an inner chamber. Here, on plinths and tables all around the room, were bowls of bronze, carved wooden chests bound in gold, and bright bells and gongs of silver.

Olly paused to gaze at the carvings on a large door at the end of the room. Inset in silver on the white stone of the door itself was a curious picture. It seemed to be a stylised depiction of the city – the high walls of the volcano were clearly shown – and from the city, a woman with shreds of cloud at her feet was flying up towards the full moon.

'It's Chang-O,' Olly murmured, her voice soft and reverent. 'This must be a temple to the moon goddess.'

Josh nodded and gently pushed the door, which swung easily open. The friends walked on into a small oval inner chamber, its pearly walls quite plain and unadorned. Over to the left, there was an altar or stone table set on four broad stone steps. A statue lay on the table, looking like the images of the dead that Olly had seen, lying on top of their own tombs as if asleep, in English churches.

But the stonework of this statue was painted in bright colours. It was a woman – dressed in red robes, her face white and her glossy black hair hanging down over the end of the altar, so long that it reached the floor. A single moonbeam shone down on to the woman's face, from a circular hole in the ceiling above her.

Olly and Josh walked silently towards the statue. As they got closer, Olly began to realise that the red silk gown and the radiant fall of black hair were not carved and painted stone at all. 'Can she be *real*?' Olly whispered in awe.

'I don't know,' Josh murmured, the confusion obvious in his voice.

They climbed the steps and looked into the beautiful face. It was white, but perfect, as though the woman had only just closed her eyes and drifted into a peaceful sleep. There was a delicate tiara of silver across her forehead, and set into the centre was a moonstone disc that shimmered with an inner light.

'She must be Chang-O,' Olly said softly. She pointed to the moonstone on the woman's forehead. 'And that must be the Mooncake,' she added. 'Josh – we've found it!'

Gently, Olly reached out and touched the moonstone. It felt slightly warm under her fingers, and it easily came free from its silver setting. Olly lifted it in the beam of bright moonlight and gazed at the surface. It was ringed with flying cranes holding trailing garlands of flowers in their beaks. In the centre was etched a crescent moon and a flaming sun.

Olly could feel Josh leaning over her shoulder. 'Should I do this?' she whispered, caught by a sudden doubt.

'I don't know,' Josh replied. 'But we can't leave it here for Ethan Cain to find.'

Olly moved the stone out of the light. Immediately the moonbeam faded and the whole room darkened. 'What's happening?' Olly asked.

Far above them, they heard a distant peal of thunder. A moment later, great heavy raindrops began to fall through the hole in the roof of the temple.

'We should go,' Josh said. He caught Olly's arm, and pulled her down the steps towards the exit.

As they neared the doorway, Olly seemed to hear a gentle sigh. She turned. Chang-O's body was surrounded by a soft glow, through which Olly could see the raindrops falling like sparkling diamonds.

And then, even as Olly watched, the glow faded and Chang-O's body crumbled to dust.

Chapter Twelve

The Storm

The thunder roared, echoing and reverberating in the crater of the ancient volcano, until Josh and Olly had to put their hands over their ears as they ran through the Moon Temple. It was darker now – not pitch black, but dark enough to make them stretch out their hands as they ran, in case they stumbled into unseen things in their path.

They came out on to the broad stone steps. The rain was falling in torrents, lashing the white stones and bouncing on the steps. The city was a dull grey now. The strange light that had made it so beautiful and unearthly had vanished, as if washed away by the rain.

A jagged fork of lightning blazed across the sky,

thunder bellowed, and the rain hammered down on the stones with a sound like hissing snakes.

'This is amazing!' Olly yelled above the noise. She ran out into the pelting rain, splashing through the puddles and stretching her arms up into the deluge. She tilted her head to let the pellets of water patter down on her face.

Josh watched from the shelter of the temple's doorway with a grin on his face. 'You're mad!' he called.

'Think of the farmers!' Olly shouted back. 'They'll be so pleased – they're all going to be OK now the rain has come. This is the best thing that could possibly have happened.'

'What about the dig?' Josh reminded her. 'It'll be washed away.'

Olly danced towards him. Her clothes were sticking to her, her hair hung in her eyes and her face was running with water, but she didn't care. 'I know,' she said, laughing and spinning in the rain, the talisman clutched tightly in one hand, 'but we've got the Mooncake now! That's the really important thing.'

Olly skipped back up the temple steps to Josh. She wiped the water out of her eyes and gazed out at the city. It was awash. Already puddles of rainwater were spreading across the stone streets. The temple was on a small hill, but all around it the ground dipped before rising again towards the crater walls. Puddles were beginning to combine into large grey pools.

A long groan of thunder shook the air.

'I think we better head back and show Jonathan and your dad what we've found,' Josh suggested.

Olly nodded and pushed the precious moonstone into her pocket. 'OK,' she said. 'Let's go!' They ran down the temple steps.

Olly had never known a storm like this – the whole world seemed full of falling water. It was cascading from roofs, streaming through the streets, gushing and spilling over statues and sculptures until it seemed as if the city was melting around them.

Lightning sizzled across the clouds with thunder at its heels. 'Isn't this the most amazing storm you've ever seen?' Olly shouted. 'I've always loved really big thunderstorms!'

Josh wiped water out of his eyes with a soaking sleeve. 'I prefer watching them from indoors,' he confessed.

Olly laughed. A tidal wave of rainwater couldn't have dampened her spirits – they had found a city, lost for thousands of years, and she had the Mooncake in her pocket. Very soon she would be able to place it in her father's hands and see the look of surprise and delight on his face. Everything was wonderful!

They turned the corner and ran back past the statues of cranes and musicians. The seated musicians were waist-deep in water now, and the birds seemed to be wading as Josh and Olly rushed on towards the stairs.

When they reached the dragon arch, they found it shrouded in fine spray, and the courtyard of soldiers beyond was half a metre deep in swirling floodwater. Josh and Olly joined hands and waded across the expanse of drowned flagstones. It was heavy going, but at last they were through the first arch and the long stone stairway rose ahead of them, water leaping and bouncing down the steps.

'Be careful,' Josh shouted as Olly began to climb.

'It'll be fine,' she called back as more thunder crashed above them.

They scrambled up into the grey clouds. There was no moonlight now to make the mist shine, and

Olly could see nothing. She felt wet, slippery rock under her feet and heard the constant splash and patter of the rain as she climbed ever upwards.

Eventually, Olly emerged above the clouds. It was a little lighter here, and above her, Olly could see the storm clouds racing across the sky. The rain was still falling, but the thunder and lightning had stopped – for a while, at least. She clambered up the last stone stairs until she came to the shelf of rock that led into the mountain.

'Thank heavens!' Josh said, staggering out of the rain and pushing his wet hair out of his eyes. 'It's crazy out there!'

Even Olly had to admit that it was a relief to be out of the battering rain. But there was a curious, roaring noise in the tunnel. She turned to Josh. 'What's that?' she asked.

'I don't know,' Josh replied. 'But I don't like the sound of it.'

The echoing rumble sounded ominous to him. He led the way along the tunnel, but as they neared the stairs, the din got louder and louder. Josh took out his torch and played the beam along the passage. He walked to the top of the stairway and listened to the noise that echoed up from the depths. He looked at Olly. 'I've got a bad feeling about this noise,' he muttered grimly.

She listened. 'It's nothing,' she said hopefully. 'Just the rain.'

'I hope you're right,' Josh replied, and together they began the long climb down to the waterway.

They had been on the stairs for only a few minutes, when the torchlight suddenly shone on dark floodwater only a couple of steps below. It filled the stairwell, heaving and churning over the steps, one by one.

Josh and Olly drew to a halt, staring down into the flood.

'Well, I don't think we can dive down and get out this time!' Olly exclaimed.

Josh nodded. 'You're right about that,' he said. 'If the water has risen this far, then the whole of the canal will be flooded, too.'

Olly blinked at him. 'So, what do we do?'

Josh turned and shone the torch back up the stairs. 'We'll have to look for another way out,' he declared.

'*Is* there one?' Olly queried.

'I don't know,' Josh replied.

They climbed the stairs in silence. For a moment,

Josh almost wished he had stayed back at camp in the warmth and comfort of his cabin. But then he thought of beautiful Yueliang-Chengshi and the moonstone safe in Olly's pocket, and he knew it would all be worth it – once they were safely out of the volcano!

The roar of the rising flood lessened as they climbed. 'I'm getting really sick of these stairs,' Olly puffed.

'Tell me about it,' Josh agreed. But at last they reached the top of the stairway. Josh looked towards the far end of the tunnel and saw a cascade of falling water. He and Olly made their way along the passage and gingerly edged out through the water on to the rain-washed ledge.

Olly turned to look up at the cliff-face above them. 'We'll never climb out that way,' she called to Josh. 'You'd need to be able to fly, like Chang-O, to get over the mountain.'

'That's it!' Josh exclaimed. At Olly's words, an image had flashed into his mind. 'Remember that picture on the door in the temple?' he reminded her. 'The one of Chang-O flying to the moon? I think it showed a route up the inside of the crater.' He looked at her. 'Another way out!'

'Are you sure?' Olly asked.

Josh nodded. 'I think so. Besides – what choice do we have? Let's go and look at it again before the water gets too high.'

Olly frowned at him. 'If we end up getting drowned down there, I'll never talk to you again!' she warned.

He smiled grimly. 'Fair enough.'

This time it was Josh who took the lead down the stairs and through the cloud bank. The silver city was afloat in a rolling ocean of water now, and the flood came up to their waists as the friends struggled to wade across the courtyard. The soldiers simply stared ahead impassively as the water rose around them.

Josh and Olly fought their way on, half-wading, half-swimming, until they could see the temple on its hill. The sight of the beautiful white building – still standing proud of the flood, on its stone steps – gave them renewed determination, and they began to make their way up the long avenue towards it.

They were almost there when, suddenly, Josh felt Olly being dragged away by the flood. She had lost her footing in the racing water, which now threatened to sweep her away entirely.

Olly's head vanished beneath the water. Josh clung on tightly to her hand, but felt his own feet losing their grip in the rising tide. Olly surfaced, coughing and gasping for air as Josh felt his feet being lifted off the ground. He lunged forwards, dragging Olly with him, in a last desperate attempt to reach the steps.

It was with huge relief that he felt stone beneath his feet again and dragged himself out of the deluge. He helped Olly to her feet, but the flood was rising swiftly now, and they had to climb another step to get away from the lapping water. Josh gazed out over the city and felt a rush of panic. The temple hill was an island in a rising sea. They had just about reached the building – but were they ever going to be able to leave it again?

Chapter Thirteen

The Man in the Demon Mask

'Well?' said Olly. 'Now what?' They stood under the shelter of the temple gateway, watching the rain falling on the drowning city.

Josh didn't reply. He stared up at the clouds for a moment, then turned and walked into the temple.

Olly stayed there beneath the arch of the doorway, holding the Mooncake in her hand. She imagined that Chang-O herself might once have stood in the very same spot, old and tired from her long hunt for her husband. Perhaps she, too, gazed out over the city, but saw it then alive and bustling with people and animals now long gone.

Olly fingered the talisman in her pocket. It still

felt curiously warm against her skin. Her brain told her that taking the talisman from Chang-O's crown could not have brought the rain – but she did feel that maybe she had been *meant* to find the Mooncake. And some strange instinct told her that she and Josh would be kept safe by it. Chang-O would watch over them, Olly thought, and then smiled to herself – imagining how Josh would react to such a fantastical idea.

'Olly!' Josh called from inside the temple.

'Yes?' Olly replied, tearing herself away from her view of the city and heading inside.

'I think I've worked it out,' Josh told her as she joined him at the door of the innermost chamber. He pointed to the picture. 'See?' he continued. 'I know where this building with the two spires is. You can see those spires in the distance from the steps outside – they're in the opposite direction from the way we came.' He traced the pathway that the long-dead artist had threaded through the city. 'If we take this direct line from here to the building with the two spires, it should lead us to the path up the mountain.' His finger came to the base of a zigzag line that led up to the mountain peaks, from which Chang-O was depicted, flying to the full moon. 'There's only one problem,' Josh finished. 'How do we get across the city?'

'We swim for it if we have to,' Olly replied.

Josh looked at her. 'You didn't enjoy it too much last time we went swimming, if you remember,' he pointed out.

Olly smiled. 'I didn't have the talisman with me, then,' she said.

Josh gave her a puzzled look.

'Everything will work out fine,' Olly told him. 'You'll see.'

They ventured out into the endless rain again and made their way around to the far side of the temple. Olly saw the building with the two spires away in the distance. It stood on a ridge of high ground above the flood. But between that building and the temple, the waters ran wild and deep, pouring into the city from many different directions, rushing and roaring through the streets.

Olly stepped down to the water's edge and stared into the torrent, gathering her courage for the plunge. Her fingers tightened on the talisman. She took a long, slow breath and stepped down again. The water swirled and boiled around her ankles. Another step, and it was up to her shins. And then

– with the third step – something astonishing happened.

Olly's foot jarred on a surface higher than she had been expecting. She stepped out again cautiously, and still the ground remained level beneath her. She turned and looked at Josh. 'There's some kind of pathway just under the water,' she told him. She stooped, trying to see the path through the troubled floodwater. She could dimly see a faint white line under the surface, and she laughed with delight, because the path seemed to be leading them straight to the building with the two spires. 'Come on in,' she called to Josh. 'The water's lovely!'

Josh grinned as he came down the steps to join Olly, and side by side, they waded out towards the two spires.

'I think the rain is beginning to ease off,' Josh said, staring up at the clouds. He looked back at the city. Water was still pouring off the roofs and cascading through the streets, but the fierceness of the downpour did seem to have lessened.

They were standing on a flat terrace of white stone that jutted out from the mountainside. Above them, a narrow path made its jagged, zigzag way up the inside of the crater. The friends had another hard climb ahead of them.

'What time do you think it is?' Olly asked.

'Midnight?' Josh suggested. 'Maybe even later.'

Olly gazed out over the city. 'I hope the water doesn't do too much damage,' she murmured. 'It's such a beautiful place.'

'It'll be a while before any excavations can be carried out,' Josh commented. 'It'll probably be weeks before all that water drains away.'

Olly turned her head sharply and stared at him.

'What?' he queried, surprised by the look on her face.

Olly shook her head. 'Nothing,' she said. 'I'd just like to get back to camp and put some dry clothes on, that's all.'

'If the camp is still there,' Josh remarked. 'With this amount of rain, the whole lot could be underwater by now. The ruins will be flooded at the very least.'

He set off up the zigzag path. Water was flowing down the track, making it slippery, but it was an easier route than the stone stairway had been. Every now and then the climb was relieved by a wide paved area. The friends rested on those high galleries, catching their breath and giving their legs time to recover.

Eventually, they came to the cloud bank. The city faded away into a grey haze beneath them and was lost from sight. 'I've got the weirdest feeling we'll never see it again,' Olly said.

Josh looked at her. 'Of course we will,' he replied. 'Once we tell Jonathan and your dad about it, they'll want us to show them the way in. The dig will probably be extended for months. There must be an incredible amount of stuff down there – enough to fill an entire museum.'

Olly just nodded thoughtfully.

They soon emerged from the cloud bank and saw again the fangs of the mountain all around them. The thunder-clouds seemed less threatening now, and the rain was much lighter, as if the storm's fury had worn itself out.

They came to a final platform. Bronze dragons guarded an ornate archway made of glowing jade. Josh took his torch out again and shone the beam through the arch and into the tunnel beyond.

'Look at this!' he exclaimed. He had expected to see a simple passageway hacked through the rock, like the one by which they had entered the city, but the torchlight was reflected by a thousand jewels, set in panels of onyx and jade and ivory that lined the entire length of the passage.

There were plinths set into the panelled walls, on which rested sculptures made of stone and bronze, silver and pottery. Josh gazed in fascination at dancing figures and long-necked birds. Horses and lions and dragons.

Josh and Olly were cold and tired and wet through, but they forgot their fatigue and discomfort as they marvelled at the ancient treasures of Yueliang-Chengshi. Josh noticed that many of the sculptures and carvings showed a man with a bow and arrows, while others seemed to depict Chang-O, either afloat in clouds or gazing up to a full moon. All along the tunnel, the walls were inlaid with representations of the moon – from crescent to full, wrought in silver and bronze and gold.

It was almost a disappointment for the friends when the torchlight showed the tunnel narrowing to a dark exit on to the mountainside. The mouth of the passage was a narrow and curved slit like a huge cat's eye.

Josh squeezed through first. He emerged about a third of the way up the mountain, and found himself staring out through fine rain over a landscape that he didn't recognise. Olly appeared at his shoulder. Below them, clustered among the foothills, was a mass of bright lights – a town.

'Is that Banping?' Olly asked.

'I don't think so,' Josh replied. 'It's too big. I think it must be Chung-Hsien.' As if to confirm his words, a rocket – trailing fire – suddenly soared up from the town and burst in a shower of gold and silver sparks. A second and a third blaze of light followed, one exploding in red fire, the other opening up like a golden flower. A few moments later, the sizzle and crackle of the fireworks reached their ears.

'It's the Moon Festival!' Olly exclaimed happily.

Josh turned to look back at the fissure through which they had emerged. He frowned. The rock-face seemed smooth and featureless with no sign of an opening. He took a step back to investigate, shining his torchbeam over the rocks.

Olly watched the fireworks for a few moments, then she turned to speak to Josh. He was gone.

'Josh?' she called. Even without the light of his torch, she could see quite well – and there was absolutely no sign of him.

'Josh!' She couldn't understand where he'd gone. A few seconds ago he had been standing right beside her. Her heart leapt into her mouth. Perhaps something had happened to him. Had the Shan-Ren taken him again? She looked around anxiously and then realised, with a jolt, that the cleft through which they had exited the tunnel had also vanished.

'Josh!' There was an edge of panic in her voice now.

'What's the matter?' Josh asked, sounding quite normal – and very close by. 'What are you yelling about?'

'Where are you?' Olly asked, staring at the rocks.

'I'm here.' Suddenly, right in front of her eyes, Josh shimmered into sight. Olly let out a yelp of surprise.

Josh was grinning from ear to ear. 'I think it must be some kind of optical illusion,' he explained. 'You can't see the way into the tunnel from the outside.' He stepped back, dissolving into thin air. A moment later, he stepped forwards and reappeared. 'See?' he said.

'Please stop doing that,' Olly begged. 'It's weird!'

'Don't you get it?' Josh asked. 'That's why this place has never been found. You'd have to know exactly where the entrance is to be able to go through it.' He frowned. 'We should leave some kind of marker here, or we won't be able to find it again.'

'Leave your torch,' Olly suggested. 'We won't need it now.'

'Good idea.' Josh switched his torch off and laid it on the ground in front of the secret entrance, so that it pointed to the hidden fissure. 'There,' he said. 'Now we'll be able to get back to the city, even if the canal is underwater again after all this rain.'

'Come on,' Olly said. 'I want to go and show Dad what we've found. And he's probably down there in Chung-Hsien.'

Josh nodded, and they set off down the mountain towards the welcoming lights of Chung-Hsien, all thoughts of exhaustion and cold forgotten.

It wasn't long before they could hear the sounds of the festival – music and laughter, and the constant hiss and roar as more fireworks were launched into the sky.

'They've really got something to celebrate now the rain has come,' Olly said elatedly. She looked slyly at Josh. 'Do you think we had anything to do with making it rain?'

He frowned at her. 'Hardly.'

Olly grinned. 'I'm not so sure,' she said. She put her hand in her pocket and touched the Mooncake. 'I think Yueliang-Chengshi is a very strange place,' she continued thoughtfully. 'And I think we were meant to find the talisman.'

Josh eyed her dubiously. 'Let's hope Jonathan and your father think the same,' he said.

Olly laughed. 'Oh, they'll forgive us for leaving camp when they see the talisman,' she said. 'I can't wait to see my dad's face! This will be two Talismans of the Moon that we've found.' She grinned at Josh. 'We'll have to write a book about—' An alarmed look on Josh's face silenced her. She turned to see what had startled him.

Two of Lau's men stood in front of them, as if they had appeared out of nowhere.

'Oh, *rats!*' Olly muttered. She and Josh both turned to run, but two more men in grey stood barring their way back. One of them was Lau himself.

'You are difficult people to find,' he remarked, his voice smooth and cold.

'We're going to see my father,' Olly told him defiantly. 'You can't stop us.'

'I think you'll find I can,' Lau retorted. He spoke briefly in Mandarin, and a moment later both Olly and Josh were held securely by Lau's guards.

Olly glared at Lau. 'If you don't take us to my father, you're going to be in a lot of trouble,' she said. 'I know who you really work for – and he doesn't scare me.'

'Please come with me,' Lau said calmly. He turned, beckoning to his men.

Olly and Josh were bundled along in Lau's wake. Olly struggled in vain. She thought of shouting for help, but the noise of the festival was too loud – she would never be heard. For the time being, she decided, they had no choice but to do what Lau wanted.

They came to a large wooden house on the outskirts of the town. Lau led them into a room lit with a rainbow of brightly-coloured lanterns. A figure in a traditional robe of blue and white silk stood with its back to them at a window, apparently watching the festivities.

Lau motioned to his men to bring Olly and Josh forward.

'Let us go!' Olly demanded, struggling again.

The figure at the window turned slowly to face her. Covering his head was a Chinese demon mask, the eyes blazing red under fiercely frowning brows, the mouth distorted into a fearsome grin that displayed pointed white fangs.

Olly and Josh stared at the apparition in shocked silence. Olly swallowed hard. 'Who are you?' she asked.

The figure raised his hands to the mask and carefully lifted it off. 'Hello, Josh. Hello, Olly,' he said pleasantly. 'This is a lovely surprise.'

Olly's head spun.

It was Ethan Cain.

Chapter Fourteen

The Dragon Dance

Olly stared at Ethan with unconcealed dislike. 'What are you doing here?' she demanded, though she had already guessed he was looking for the Mooncake of Chang-O.

Ethan nodded towards the window. 'I came to watch the Festival of the Moon,' he replied. He gestured towards the mask. 'And to join in with the festivities a little, in my own way.' He smiled at them, but Olly saw a ruthless gleam in his eyes. 'The lion dance is intended to bring on the rain,' he commented. 'Did you know?'

'Yes,' Josh snapped.

The American half-turned to the window again, and traced a raindrop down the glass with one finger. 'It seems to have worked,' he remarked. 'Very nice for the local farmers – but something of a blow for your father, Olly, I should think. I don't imagine he's even close to finding the talisman yet.' He smiled. 'I wonder if you've had more luck.' His gaze flicked to Josh. 'Luck was obviously with you when you found that golden disc.'

'We're not frightened of you,' Josh stated defiantly.

Ethan raised an eyebrow in an expression of puzzlement and surprise. 'What an extraordinary thing to say, Josh,' he said mildly.

'*You* stole the disc!' Olly spat. 'It was you all along.'

He gave a dismissive wave of his hand. 'I didn't steal it.' He looked from Olly to Josh. 'What do you know about the Shan-Ren? I was under the impression that they had died out – but their name keeps popping up.' His eyes narrowed. 'Do they still exist?'

'As if we'd tell you!' Olly declared scornfully. 'We know you put up the money for this dig – and you deliberately used a fake name so nobody would know it was you.'

The American grimaced, as though hurt. 'Why

do you persist in misunderstanding me?' he asked. 'I have a fascination for archaeology. I kept my own name out of the proceedings merely to prevent media interest. The Chinese authorities didn't want swarms of reporters descending on the site, so they asked that I remain anonymous.' He smiled at Josh. 'Being the son of a celebrity, I'm sure you know how inconvenient it can be to have a high media profile.'

Josh didn't reply.

'We know exactly why you're here,' Olly muttered darkly. Then she let out a harsh laugh. 'And you're too late, so you might just as well turn around and go straight back home again!'

With the speed of a striking snake, Ethan glided across the floor to Olly's side. 'What do you mean, I'm too late?' he demanded icily.

'She meant the rain will close down the dig,' Josh put in. 'That's all she meant.'

Ethan Cain fixed Olly with a piercing gaze. She lifted her chin, and looked him boldly in the eyes, her mouth set in a determined line.

'Did she mean that?' Ethan mused in a low whisper as he stared at Olly. 'Or did she mean something else entirely?'

A shiver of unease ran through Olly. She had the horrible feeling that he had guessed the real meaning of her words. She could feel the talisman heavy in her pocket. All he had to do was search her and he'd have it.

She held his gaze for a long time, and it was Ethan who looked away first. He turned and walked back to the window. Olly glanced quickly over her shoulder. Lau and his men stood behind her, blocking the way to the door.

'What were you doing on the mountain?' Ethan asked quietly, still with his back to the friends.

'We went for a little walk,' Josh replied.

'No,' Cain said flatly. 'You made up your beds to give the impression that you were still at the camp, and then you left without being seen.' He looked at Olly. 'Your grandmother had told you to stay put,' he murmured thoughtfully. 'Mrs Beckmann is a formidable woman. You wouldn't have disobeyed her without good reason. I believe that Josh saw something on the golden disc that sent you out on the mountain – twice – without permission. I think it was something to do with the old stream, because that's where Lau lost track of you the first time. And I suspect you were looking for something. My guess is that you thought you had a clue that would lead to the Mooncake of Chang-O.' He wheeled around suddenly. 'You're both resourceful people, I remember that from our little disagreement in Egypt. So were you lucky, I wonder?' he continued. 'Did you find it? Or something that would lead you to it?'

Olly exchanged glances with Josh. They both knew better than to say anything. A few tense moments passed.

'I'd like to go and find my father now, if that's OK with you,' Olly said calmly, breaking the silence.

A flash of anger crossed the American's face. 'Search them!' he ordered.

Olly turned to see Lau and his men moving forwards. But, suddenly, the window shattered and the air was full of broken glass. Ethan threw his arms up to protect his face just in time, as fragments of glass flew around him. And there was something else – something that shot across the room, trailing smoke. It came crashing to the floor at Lau's feet.

He stared down at it for a moment. And then an explosion of white light and noise sent him staggering backwards. The thing had split into burning, sparking fragments which began to career wildly around the room, giving off ear-splitting shrieks and bangs.

Olly realised what it was – someone had thrown a bundle of large firecrackers in through the window. She grabbed hold of Josh's hand and together they ran for the door. Josh snatched it open and slammed it shut behind them. They raced along the corridor towards the main entrance of the building. They could hear pounding feet behind them – Lau's men were already in the corridor. And above the continued explosions from the firecrackers, they could also hear Ethan Cain shouting commands.

Reaching the front door, they leapt from the building and plunged down an alleyway. 'Who threw the firework?' Josh gasped.

'I didn't see,' Olly said. 'I don't know.'

They rounded a corner, their feet slipping on wet earth. A long passageway between two buildings led to a brightly-lit street. They ran towards it.

But a figure melted out of the shadows in front of them, barring their path. They slithered to a halt. The man was dressed in red and across the lower half of his face he wore a red scarf. On the scarf was the now-familiar Shan-Ren pictogram.

The man pointed to one side, and spoke urgently in Mandarin. Olly saw that there was a narrow open door in the wooden wall. She didn't have time to think it through – but she had a hunch that the man was trying to help them, so she dived through the doorway with Josh only an instant behind.

The man followed and shut the door. The room was in darkness, lit only by the light that filtered in between the wooden slats of the wall. Their rescuer stood silent and alert with his back to the door, listening.

They heard running feet in the alley getting closer and then running on past.

The man let out a sigh of relief and then spoke again in Mandarin.

'*Wo bu dong*,' Olly replied. I don't understand.

A sudden light illuminated the room. The man held a torch in his hand. He untied the scarf from around his face and smiled at Olly and Josh as he let out another stream of Mandarin. Olly liked the man's face, he looked honest and kind. He smiled again and pressed his hands together, bowing slightly.

'I think he's on our side,' Josh whispered.

The man held his hands up, making a circle with his fingers. 'Chang-O,' he said. He looked from Olly to Josh. 'Chang-O.'

'Yes,' Olly agreed, moved by a sudden sense of understanding. 'Yes – Chang-O!' She put her hand in her pocket and drew out the Mooncake. 'We found it in the old city in the mountain,' she explained. 'The Shan-Ren have been keeping the city a secret for thousands of years, haven't they?'

The man gazed at the moonstone then looked enquiringly at Olly, as if trying to understand what she was saying. 'And now we've found it,' she added thoughtfully. 'And soon the whole place will be full of strangers.' She frowned. 'It's all wrong,' she said decisively, turning to Josh. 'We shouldn't do this.'

Josh frowned. 'What do you mean?'

'The old city has been kept secret for so long, Josh,' she replied. 'We can't tell. It would be wrong.'

'You mean we shouldn't tell *anyone*?' Josh queried. 'Not even Jonathan and your dad?'

Olly gave him a crooked smile. 'Is that crazy?' she asked. She wasn't sure where her thoughts were coming from. She just had an image in her mind of the beautiful old city being ransacked by greedy men like Ethan Cain. She turned back to her Chinese rescuer. 'Did you throw that firework into the room?'

The man stared at her blankly. Olly did a pantomime of the firework banging and leaping around. '*Ni?*' she asked. You? The man smiled and nodded.

Hardly understanding why she did it, Olly suddenly held the Mooncake of Chang-O out to the man from the Shan-Ren. 'Take it,' she said. 'Put it back where it came from.'

The man shook his head. He reached out and closed Olly's hand around the moonstone, pushing it away from him. He carefully replaced the scarf over his mouth and nose, and opened the door on to the alley. Then he gestured for them to leave.

As they stepped out into the fine rain, he put a hand on Josh's shoulder. Olly saw something being pressed into Josh's hand, then the door closed on the man and they stood alone in the alley.

Josh held the object up. It was a torch.

'Why did he give you that?' Olly asked.

Josh was looking at it with an extraordinary

expression on his face. He looked up at her. 'Because it's mine,' he said simply.

Olly looked confused and Josh gave a breath of laughter. 'It's my torch, Olly,' he explained. 'The one we left on the mountain – to mark the passage.'

'Oh!'

'I don't think he wants us to find our way back to the city,' Josh mused.

'But he let us keep the Mooncake,' Olly said bemusedly. 'What does it mean?'

'I *think* it means that the Shan-Ren are OK with us finding the talisman, but that they don't want the city disturbed,' Josh said. 'I agree with you – we mustn't tell anyone about it. We can say we found the talisman in the watercourse.'

Olly lifted the moonstone. 'Let's go and find Dad,' she said. 'The quicker this is somewhere safe, the happier I'll be.'

They made their way to the end of the alley and came out into the brightly-lit street. It was filled with revellers and noise, and hung with lanterns and streamers. Food and drink were being sold from colourful wooden stalls, musicians were playing traditional tunes and people were dancing in the muddy streets, delighted that the rain had come.

Fireworks were still going off all over town. Rockets shot into the sky and exploded in coloured fire. Firecrackers jumped and whirled with flashes and bangs. And showers of silver, green and gold sparks streamed down from upper windows.

Olly caught a glimpse of one of Lau's men in the throng. He was speaking on a mobile phone. He didn't seem to have noticed them. Quickly, she caught hold of Josh's arm and pulled him in the opposite direction.

The two friends darted through the revellers, constantly on the lookout for pursuit. Olly saw another of Lau's men on the far side of the street. Before she could duck out of sight he spotted her and reached for his phone. She slipped behind a stall. 'They've seen us,' she said to Josh.

He nodded. 'I know – and there's one over there, too.' He pointed to a corner where another security man was standing, scanning the crowd for the two friends.

Olly and Josh slipped away down a side road. They emerged in a central square which was so crowded they could only just push their way through the throng. The bamboo houses surrounding the square were strung with glowing lanterns and the music here was loud and very rhythmic.

Josh wiggled his way to the front of the crowd, with Olly hanging on to his shirt so they wouldn't get separated. A dragon dance was taking place. The great creature swayed and writhed across the square, chasing a masked man in a vivid red costume, who bounded athletically ahead of the monster, performing cartwheels and somersaults. The dragon's head was beautifully made with golden horns, snapping red jaws and a long golden beard. Its eyes rolled and swivelled as it chased the man in red, while drums thundered and cymbals crashed.

Under the flowing silken body and tail, Olly could make out at least ten pairs of legs, expertly following the intricate choreography of the dance as the great beast swept around the square, its head rising and falling to the rhythm of the drums.

Mesmerised, Olly watched the man in red veer away as the dragon almost caught him. The fearsome creature wheeled and sped after him, its body undulating as if it were alive, trailing long silk streamers from its horns and ears and tail.

Olly was so absorbed by the rhythm of the

dragon's movements, that she didn't notice Lau approaching until he put his hand on her neck. She started violently, then squirmed free and tumbled out into the square, pulling Josh with her.

The masked man saw them and ran forwards, gesticulating wildly, shouting and leaping. Olly scrambled to her feet and looked around frantically. She saw Lau making his way towards her through the crowd, and more of his men closing in from other directions. There was no way out.

The masked man grabbed Olly's wrist and dragged her towards the middle of the square. She struggled, and Josh ran to rescue her, but the man caught his arm, too. He spoke from behind the mask. 'Go to the dragon,' he said in English with a heavy Chinese accent. 'He will protect you. Go!'

There were shouts and calls and cheers from the crowd as the masked man led Olly and Josh towards the dragon. It was coiled in the middle of the square now, writhing and rolling its eyes.

Dazed and bewildered, Olly allowed herself to be pushed towards the dragon's snapping jaws. At the same time the body and tail came snaking around her and Josh, effectively blocking Lau and his men from reaching them. A section of the silk that formed the dragon's body lifted high and the friends found themselves drawn in under the bamboo framework.

A gong sounded. The dragon roared and began to move. Olly saw that Josh had caught hold of the dancer directly ahead of him, and was trying to mimic the man's movements. She did the same, doing her best to follow the path of the dragon dance. She couldn't see what was going on – her whole world consisted of the black-clad dancers and the bamboo frame with its covering of coloured silk. But somehow she managed to keep in step as they took a zigzag course across the square.

She heard shouts and laughter and saw the feet of spectators as they ran from the dragon. She realised they were at the far side of the square now. The dancer directly behind Olly spoke briefly and pushed her. She and Josh came stumbling out from under the dragon's skirts and were quickly absorbed into the crowd.

'Were they Shan-Ren?' Josh gasped, breathless from the wild dance.

'I don't know,' Olly panted. 'But they got us away from Lau, whoever they were.'

'Let's find your dad,' Josh said. 'Before Lau catches up with us again.'

They made their way through the festive streets, desperate to catch sight of Jonathan or the professor. Smiling vendors offered them mooncakes and hedgehog buns and fresh noodles, but they had no time to enjoy the sights and sounds of the festival. Olly just wanted the talisman to be safe. And Lau's men seemed to be everywhere, while there was no sign of anyone from the camp.

'Maybe we should find somewhere to hide?' Josh suggested. 'Just till things quieten down. If they can't find us, maybe Lau's men will think we've gone back to the dig site.'

Olly nodded. 'Good idea,' she said. 'It's got to be better than running around until we get caught again.' She stopped and looked about her. They were in a narrow alley, cluttered with bicycles and bins and even several baskets of chickens. 'How about this place?' she suggested.

'Why not?' Josh agreed. 'We could duck down behind the baskets and just lie low till the festival is over.'

'I think we'll be safe here,' Olly said, heading over to the baskets Josh had indicated. She took the Mooncake of Chang-O out of her pocket, feeling again its curious warmth in her hand. 'Ethan won't get his hands on the talisman now.'

'I'm not so sure,' Josh replied in a low voice.

Olly turned back towards him, and saw five of Lau's men approaching from the end of the alley. 'Run!' Olly yelled. She swung round, prepared to make a dash for it, but a figure blocked her way – a figure with outstretched arms, dressed in a long blue and white robe. Olly stared up into the fiendish grin of a demon mask.

Ethan Cain had them trapped.

Chapter Fifteen

The Keepers of the Great Secret

Ethan stepped forwards and stretched out his hand. 'I'll take that, thank you, Olivia,' he said.

Olly and Josh shrank together in the narrow street. Only a short distance away, they could see the bright lights and hear the joyful music of the continuing festival, but with Ethan in front of them and Lau's men behind, there was no escape.

Olly realised that she still had the talisman in her hand. The white moonstone glowed between her fingers. 'No!' she shouted breathlessly. 'You can't have it!'

The American grabbed Olly's arm. She twisted in his grip, struggling to break free. And then her feet slipped on the wet ground, she lost her balance and the talisman flew from her fingers.

It arced through the fine rain, shining like a miniature moon. Olly watched in silent dismay, as a figure stepped around the corner of the narrow street and instinctively caught the object that came hurtling towards him. The moonstone landed squarely in his palm and he closed his fingers around it. Olly looked up at the newcomer's face, and her eyes widened in surprise. It was her father!

Professor Christie stared in complete astonishment at the moonstone disc that had fallen into his hand. And Olly tore herself loose from Ethan Cain and ran to him. 'It's the talisman,' she shouted joyously. 'It's the Mooncake of Chang-O! We found it. Josh and I found it!'

More men appeared from around the corner. One was Doctor Feng, but there were other Chinese men with them that Olly and Josh had never seen before.

'Good heavens, Olivia, what do you mean?' the professor asked in bewilderment.

'Look at it, Dad!' Olly told him.

The professor peered at the moonstone and his face lit up with surprise and delight. 'I think it is,' he gasped. 'Olivia – where on earth did you find this?'

'We were searching the canal,' Josh put in hurriedly.

The professor stared at him. 'The canal? You mean the old waterway?' He gazed at the talisman, then at Olly and Josh. 'Good heavens,' he said again, clearly lost for words.

Doctor Feng and the other men crowded around to look at the talisman. And Ethan Cain took off his mask and stepped forwards, his face wreathed in smiles. 'Professor Christie,' he said. 'So nice to see you again – and at such a moment!'

Olly caught a fleeting glimpse of suppressed anger and greed in Ethan's eyes – but a second later it was gone, hidden behind the fake smile.

Looking a little dazed, Professor Christie shook the American's outstretched hand. 'Ethan!' he exclaimed. 'What brings you here?'

'I have a confession to make, Professor,' Cain said. 'I'm the man co-funding the excavation of the ruins. As soon as I heard about the accident, I dropped everything to come and visit Professor Andryanova in hospital, and to see how things were going.' He smiled. 'I never hoped to arrive on the very day that the Mooncake of Chang-O was discovered!'

192

Josh and Olly exchanged glances. They knew better than to try and reveal Ethan's real motives for turning up – he would talk his way out of any accusations, and they would just end up looking stupid.

'Where's Jonathan, Professor?' Josh asked.

Professor Christie had pulled an eye-glass from his pocket and was minutely examining the moonstone. He was so absorbed by the talisman that Josh asked twice without getting a response.

'Your brother went back to camp to check that everything was all right,' Doctor Feng eventually told him. 'The rain was so heavy we thought the camp might be in danger of flooding. Mrs Beckmann went with him.' His eyebrows rose as he smiled at Josh and Olly. 'I believe she intended to relent of her punishment and allow you to come to the Moon Festival. She will be worried that you are not in your cabins. Perhaps I should call her and let her know that you are safe and sound.'

'Oh.' Olly's face reddened. 'Yes – would you, please? And don't forget to tell her about the talisman.'

Doctor Feng stepped to one side and took out his mobile phone.

Olly looked at Josh. 'Gran will forgive us when she hears that we found the Mooncake of Chang-O,' she whispered. 'Won't she?'

Josh nodded, smiling. 'You mean she'll probably only half kill us.'

'Something like that.'

Ethan had moved across to speak with the Chinese men who accompanied Olly's father. One of the men was interpreting, and from what Olly could make out, they were officials from Chengdu who had come to confer with her father and to check on the dig in the wake of the accident.

Olly listened in disgust as the American smooth-talked the Chinese officials. 'That guy is such a creep,' she muttered to Josh. 'If only they knew the truth about him!'

'Tell me about it!' Josh growled. Olly looked at him sympathetically. She knew that he had more reason than her to loathe the charming Californian billionaire. Josh glowered at Ethan. 'It's not much fun knowing my mother is dating a total sleaze-ball!' he murmured under his breath.

Their subdued conversation was interrupted by the sudden arrival of Jonathan. He was out of breath and anxious. 'It's not good back at the camp,

Professor,' he said. 'The river is already rising.' Then he caught sight of the moonstone talisman in Professor Christie's hands. 'What . . .?' he gasped.

Josh ran up to him. 'It's the Mooncake of Chang-O!' he said proudly. 'Olly and I found it.'

Jonathan looked hard at the two friends. 'You should call your gran, Olly – right now. She's frantic with worry about you.'

'Doctor Feng is calling her,' Olly muttered sheepishly. 'I'll make it up to her.'

Jonathan turned back to gaze at the Mooncake. 'Where did you find it? *How* did you find it?'

'We followed the course of the canal,' Josh explained. 'And there it was! It was just luck, really.'

Olly noticed that Josh was carefully avoiding telling any direct lies. 'The place where we found it is probably underwater by now,' she added. She glanced at Josh. 'It was dark and we couldn't really see where we were. I don't think we'd be able to find the same place again.'

Josh nodded his agreement.

Doctor Feng joined them. 'I have spoken with Mrs Beckmann,' he reported. 'She says she is glad that you are both safe and sound, but she has a few words to say to you about your midnight wanderings!'

'Did she sound angry?' Olly asked.

Doctor Feng shook his head. 'She was more concerned with supervising the evacuation of the camp. But she said you are not to leave Professor Christie's side under any circumstances.'

'That's fine by us,' Josh said with a grin.

The professor held the talisman up between his fingers. 'It's a wonderful piece of craftsmanship,' he said. 'I believe there are pictograms among the engraved pictures. We must get them translated as soon as possible.' Then his face clouded and he looked at Doctor Feng. 'Did you say the camp was being evacuated?'

'That's right,' Jonathan confirmed. 'The river is already rising. The water was only a metre or so from the lower huts when I left. Olly's gran stayed behind with some of the team to start moving things to higher ground. I think we'll have time to rescue everything, but the ruins are already suffering. The lower pits are full of water, and if the river keeps rising at its current rate, I'm afraid the whole site will be underwater by morning.'

'The farmers must be happy, though,' Olly

pointed out, seeing the disappointment on her father's face. 'And we *have* found another Talisman of the Moon.'

The professor nodded. 'Yes, you're quite right, Olivia. We mustn't be selfish – the rain is a real blessing. And we can thank our lucky stars that we have the talisman – and a great many other priceless artefacts.'

Olly could feel Ethan's eyes on her. She turned and smiled at him. 'It's great, isn't it, Mr Cain?' she said innocently. 'I bet you're delighted that my father has the talisman.'

He smiled suavely back at her. 'You know exactly how delighted I am, Olly.'

Olly looked him squarely in the eyes. 'Yes,' she said. 'I do.'

Usually the Festival of the Moon in Chung-Hsien began to wind down at midnight, but not tonight. The people from the town, the local villages and the farms were far too excited to let the celebrations stop. After months of drought and uncertainty, the rain had come. The mighty Minjiang would soon flow at full strength again and all would be well.

Olly's dad had given the friends permission to wander the streets with Ang-Lun, watching the dancers and musicians, and buying sweet mooncakes to munch as they walked happily among the noisy crowd.

It was well past midnight when Ang-Lun took them to see his grandmother again. The elderly lady was sitting on a low stool near a trio of musicians who played a lilting theme on traditional Chinese instruments. Ang-Lun told the friends the names of the strange instruments: the *ruan* – a moon-shaped four-string lute; the *zhong-hu* – a long-necked, two-stringed violin; and the *di-tsu* – a bamboo flute.

The rippling music formed a gentle backdrop to their conversation with Ang-Lun's grandmother. The old lady seemed delighted to see Olly and Josh, taking their hands and smiling and nodding at them as she drew them down to sit with her. She poured them some green tea, still chattering away in Mandarin.

Ang-Lun listened and translated. At first, she only seemed to be speaking about the miracle of the rain, but then Ang-Lun looked at Olly and Josh curiously, and Olly thought she caught the word

'Shan-Ren' in the tumble of incomprehensible Mandarin.

'What did she say?' Josh asked.

'I don't really understand what she means,' Ang-Lun replied slowly. 'She wants me to thank you for keeping the secret.' He shook his head. 'I don't know what she means – and she won't explain – but she says that you are now the Keepers of the Great Secret. She says you have done a good thing.'

Olly looked into Song-Ai-Mi's wise face and saw a brightness and a knowingness in her eyes. '*Xiexie*,' Olly said in her faltering Mandarin. '*Xiexie*.' Thank you. Thank you.

The old lady smiled and took Olly's hand, speaking softly as she leant over the upturned palm.

'My grandmother wishes to tell your fortune,' Ang-Lun explained.

'Am I going to be rich and famous?' Olly asked curiously.

The old lady spoke rapidly.

'My grandmother says you will have an exciting life,' Ang-Lun told Olly. 'But she says that you must beware a dangerous enemy. She also says you will have many adventures and that a good friend will always be with you.'

Olly looked at Josh. 'That'll be you,' she said with a grin. She turned again to Ang-Lun. 'Could you ask her whether we'll find any more Talismans of the Moon?'

A few moments later, Ang-Lun translated his grandmother's reply. 'She says that very soon you will fly over wide oceans and tall mountains to a lost city in a faraway land.'

'Wow!' Olly said. 'That sounds great! And will we find the next talisman there?'

The old lady laughed as Ang-Lun translated Olly's question.

Ang-Lun smiled. 'She says that only the gods can answer that question.'

Their conversation was brought to a sudden halt by the screech and roar of fireworks. A hundred rockets had been sent soaring into the night sky, where they exploded into shining flowers of sparkling silver light. Everyone watched, mesmerised, as glittering white fire rained down over the rooftops in a spectacular finale to the Festival of the Autumn Moon.

The fireworks marked the perfect end to their mission, Olly thought. The Mooncake of Chang-O had been found, the rain had come at last, and – if

Ang-Lun's grandmother was right – it sounded like it wouldn't be long before they were off on a quest for the next Talisman of the Moon.

Olly sighed happily as she gazed up into the glittering sky. She couldn't wait!

The Amulet of Quilla

Olly Christie and Josh Welles are travelling the world with Olly's father, Professor Christie, on a search for the precious Talismans of the Moon. But danger lurks in the shadows. Can Josh and Olly outwit whoever is trying to get there first?

The search for more Talismans of the Moon leads Olly and Josh deep into the jungles of South America, this time looking for the missing Amulet of Quilla. But they must brave rockfalls, flames and the mysterious riddles of the Incas to reach the Amulet – and will they get there before it falls into the wrong hands?